CLASSROOM OF THE ELITE

NOVEL 8

ASAHINA NAZUNA

A second-year, Class A student involved with Nagumo.

NAGUMO MIYABI

Class A's second-year representative. He hasn't been student council president long, but his actions and words have already proven provocative.

KIRIYAMA IKUTO

A second-year Class B student and vice president of the student council. He dropped down to Class B after losing the election to Nagumo but continues to serve under him.

CLASS C AND CLASS D MINGLING

SHIINA HIYORI

YAMASHITA SAKI

YABU NANAMI

WANG MEI-YU

KATSURAGI KOUHEI

KANZAKI RYUUJI

RYUUEN KAKERU

YOUSUKE | HIRATA

ROKUSUKE | KOUENJI

KIYOTAKA | AYANOKOUJI

CLASSROOM OF THE ELITE
NOVEL 8

CONTENTS

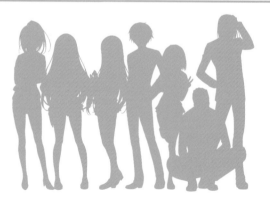

CLASSROOM OF THE ELITE

NOVEL 8

STORY BY
Syougo Kinugasa

ART BY
Tomoseshunsaku

Seven Seas Entertainment

CLASSROOM OF THE ELITE VOL. 8
YOUKOSO JITSURYOKUSHIJOUSHUGI NO KYOUSHITSU E VOL. 8
© Syougo Kinugasa 2018
Art by Tomoseshunsaku
First published in Japan in 2018 by KADOKAWA CORPORATION, Tokyo.
English translation rights arranged with KADOKAWA CORPORATION, Tokyo.

Seven Seas press and purchase enquiries can be sent to
Marketing Manager Lianne Sentar at press@gomanga.com.
Information regarding the distribution and purchase of
digital editions is available from Digital Manager CK Russell
at digital@gomanga.com.

Follow Seven Seas Entertainment online at
sevenseasentertainment.com.

TRANSLATION: Timothy MacKenzie
ADAPTATION: Jessica Cluess
COVER DESIGN: Nicky Lim
INTERIOR LAYOUT & DESIGN: Clay Gardner
PROOFREADER: Meg van Huygen, Stephanie Cohen
LIGHT NOVEL EDITOR: Nibedita Sen
PREPRESS TECHNICIAN: Rhiannon Rasmussen-Silverstein
PRODUCTION MANAGER: Lissa Pattillo
MANAGING EDITOR: Julie Davis
ASSOCIATE PUBLISHER: Adam Arnold
PUBLISHER: Jason DeAngelis

ISBN: 978-1-64827-223-3
Printed in Canada
First Printing: June 2021
10 9 8 7 6 5 4 3 2 1

1 HORIKITA MANABU'S SOLILOQUY

THERE ARE THINGS people would be surprised to discover—for example, that I didn't choose to attend this school to satisfy any burning ambitions. I'd always tried to excel, but in an aimless sort of way. I didn't know what I truly wanted out of life. I didn't aspire to be a politician, a doctor, a researcher, or anything else.

For better or worse, I liked to avoid drama. I spent my days working, indifferent and detached, merely focused upon completing the tasks assigned to me.

Setting an "example."

Being a "role model."

I believed that this was the right thing to do. However, Nagumo Miyabi continues to take direct action against me, trying to clear me from his path. Perhaps 'a bulldozer' is the description that fits him best.

As a matter of fact, I'd given up on taking action against him by the time graduation neared. I'd also never actually *tried* to make a friend whom I could truly trust from the bottom of my heart. Such things were still foreign to me.

At the end of those three years, though, it finally hit me. I realized my mistake—and the regret that it had left me with.

And, I realized, that this was just the beginning.

2 A NEW SPECIAL EXAM: MIXED TRAINING CAMP

ON A THURSDAY MORNING, shortly after the start of the third semester, several buses traveled in a row down the highway. The buses carried not only first-year students, but second- and third-year as well—the entire school jointly embarking on one big road trip.

The bus that carried us—the first-year Class C students—entered a tunnel. My ears were assaulted by the pressure change.

This was the second time I'd ridden a bus since enrolling at this school. No one had explained where we were headed or what we were doing. All we knew was that we had to wear jerseys, and it was strongly recommended we pack several spare jerseys and changes of underwear before we left. This didn't sound like a vacation, though.

Since the bus ride was about three hours or so, everyone had brought along fun items considered acceptable by the school. Cell phones were a given, but people had also brought books, playing cards, and snacks and juice. Some had even brought along game consoles.

Our seats were designated, with our names written on them, and I was seated next to Ike Kanji. I'd intended to get along with him when I enrolled here, but our relationship was still at the "just fellow classmates" stage, and opportunities to hang out with him had decreased dramatically. Instead of talking to me, his literal seatmate, he knelt on his seat, turned around, and had a loud conversation with Sudou and Yamauchi, who were seated further away.

I occasionally heard the girls tell them off for being annoying, but they didn't pay much mind. It was uproarious in here, anyway, so it was no wonder that they weren't holding back. I felt a bit lonely, but there was nothing I could do about it.

On the bright side...the recent round of exams had let me grow closer to students like Akito and Keisei.

The atmosphere on the bus was pleasant, but I could tell this wouldn't be a mere field trip. If we'd done this in the middle of winter vacation, I might have held out hope of it being just a fun outing, but the third semester was already underway. It would probably be for us to anticipate an exam like the one we'd had on the deserted island, just so we could prepare ourselves mentally. It wasn't as though Ike and the others hadn't matured at *all* since then. Probably.

Chabashira observed the students doing as they pleased with a look of deep interest. She stood close to the driver, rather near my seat, as she stared at us. Since I didn't want our gazes to meet, I decided to stare out the window. This was a long tunnel. It'd been two or three minutes since we entered.

Just as I thought that, it began to get brighter. We'd made it through.

Chabashira, who had been waiting for us to emerge from the tunnel, started to move. At the same time, the pain in my ears increased.

"Sorry to interrupt your enthusiasm, but be quiet," she said, addressing the students through a hand-held microphone. "I thought you might like to know where this bus is headed, and also what you'll be doing once we arrive."

"Well, yeah, 'course we're curious. We're not going to another deserted island, are we?" asked Ike.

Chabashira answered quickly. "I see that special exam is still seared into your collective memory. Allow me to give you some peace of mind; we don't hold special exams on that grand a scale very often. Nor are we so cruel as to put you through something like that when it's no longer summer. However, as you can already guess, there *is* a new special exam ahead. Compared to the island, though, you'll be in significantly better living conditions."

So she said—but I didn't trust her. The island aside, every special exam we'd faced so far had been insanely difficult from an average student's perspective. Hanging over our heads was the ultimate penalty of failing one of these special exams: expulsion.

"Now, the special exam that you Class D students will—"

Chabashira paused. My classmates smiled with a touch of pride as, immediately after, she bowed her head in apology.

"I'm sorry. You are Class C now. Allow me to give you newly promoted students an overview of the special exam."

Having been formally promoted to Class C in the third semester, our class seemed to be trying its best to calmly face the upcoming exam. Receiving an explanation of how that special exam worked on the bus meant we could prepare countermeasures, or at least *try* to. We couldn't just get up and walk around while the bus was in motion, but the bus was small enough that everyone could hear you if you spoke, and we could always use our phones to correspond privately with specific people.

Ike and the other noisemakers shut up, listening to what Chabashira had to say. Proof that they *had* matured, if only a little.

"We are taking you to a school camp in the mountains. We will arrive in just under an hour. The less time I have to spend explaining, the more time you'll have to strategize," said Chabashira.

An hour until the exam started, huh? In other words, if it took twenty minutes to explain the rules, we'd have forty minutes left over to plan.

"Don't students normally attend school camps and stuff in the summer?" asked Ike, who used to be a boy scout. He knew quite a bit about the mountain range we could currently see from our seats as we traveled down the highway. It was covered in white snow, even now.

"Please be quiet and listen. Remember, this is the only time you have," Chabashira rebuked, but she sounded gentle, rather than angry. Ike scratched his head sheepishly and apologized. A brief moment of laughter ensued.

School camp. I'd never heard of it, so I looked it up on my phone.

"Typically held in the summer months on days when the weather is nice. Commonly held in locations where greenery is abundant, such as the mountains. Group activities are conducted with the express purpose of promoting the

development of healthy bodies. Can also refer to an educational facility."

Just as Ike had said, it sounded like these school camps were usually held in the summer. Clearly, however, they could also take place any time of year.

"Normally, opportunities to connect with senior students are few and far between, especially for those not involved in club activities. At this school camp, you'll participate in inter-class group activities for eight days and seven nights, making this a step beyond the Sports Festival. The name we've given this special exam is the 'Mixed Camp.' Since I'm sure a verbal explanation won't satisfy you, I'll be distributing printed materials now," Chabashira continued.

She handed a stack of printouts to the students sitting in the front row, who each took one and then passed the rest back. The syllabus consisted of about twenty pages. Since she hadn't specifically told us not to look, I began to flip through it.

There were clear photographs of what I assumed to be the camp, including the dormitories, public baths, cafeteria, and so on. It was actually kind of exciting to look at these; I felt like I was paging through a travel guide. The all-important words *special exam*, however, curbed our enthusiasm.

Still, this was twenty pages of documentation on top of a verbal explanation. We'd only received a brief verbal explanation for the Paper Shuffle, which meant this exam was probably shaping up to be pretty annoying.

After confirming that everyone had received the hand-outs, Chabashira resumed speaking.

"Feel free to keep reading, but I'm going to explain the Mixed Camp now. These materials will be re-collected before you get off the bus, so please make sure you clearly understand the rules. Questions will be accepted at the end, so pay attention. Do you understand?" asked Chabashira, looking at Ike as she spoke.

Ike nodded.

"The main goal of the Mixed Camp is to foster your mental development. In order to accomplish this, we're going to start with the fundamentals of participation in civilized society—ensuring you can build stable relation-ships with people you don't know very well. Each and every one of you will learn these skills."

So that was why they were making us do group activi-ties with senior students, huh?

As Chabashira had just said, students who were in clubs might have already developed relationships with their juniors or seniors. Even so, those interactions were mostly limited to the club activities themselves. As for students who *weren't* in any clubs, hardly any of us had interacted with upperclassmen at all. You might think the school would want us to fraternize voluntarily, without need for exams or club activities to serve as incentive. Of course, it wasn't that simple in reality.

So, how did they plan to get the upperclassmen involved in this? Unless the need for direct contact was a high priority, most students would probably keep their distance from one another, just like we had during the Sports Festival. Well, we *were* headed into the mountains to a place designated as a camp, so that might be easier said than done...

At any rate, if the rules for the special exam weren't set in stone, it should be easy to find loopholes. There was a marked difference in maturity, both physically and mentally, between first- and second-year students. A year is a significant period of time in the life of a teenager. I couldn't say how extreme the gulf would prove to be, but the reality of the situation was that we wouldn't be on a level playing field.

"Once we arrive at our destination, we will divide you by gender. Next, we'll hold a school-wide discussion with all grade levels and then further divide you into six groups."

"Divide men and women, then make six groups..."

muttered Ike, as though he were trying to memorize the information.

Chabashira continued, "The minimum and maximum numbers of people in each group have already been decided. Take a good look at the guidelines on page 5 of your handout."

The students all looked at once.

Group numbers are calculated based on the total number of students, then separated by grade and gender. For instance, if there are 60 or more male students in the same grade level, the minimum number of participants in a group is 8, and the upper limit 13. If the total is 70 or more, the limits are 9 and 14. If the total is 80 or more, the limits are 10 and 15. However, in the event the number of students is under 60, please refer to a separate table.

Let's assume the ratio of boys to girls in a class didn't vary between grade levels. If there were 40 students in one class, with a boys to girls ratio of 1:1—20 boys and 20 girls—then that meant, basically, that there were a total of 80 boys across the four classes of a single grade level. That would mean between 10 and 15 people per group, with a total of six groups overall. But the fact that the syllabus referenced the total number of students first meant that these numbers would change depending on how many people had been expelled across all grade levels.

"You're probably already aware of this, but sorting you into six groups divided by gender means that students from different classes will be mixed together. For the duration of the test, your group members will be your allies. You'll be in the same boat, as it were."

"Isn't it kinda ridiculous to ask us to be in groups with people from other classes? I mean, they're our enemies," muttered Ike loud enough so that Chabashira could hear him.

He'd probably been unable to contain himself any longer. But his own words must have jogged something in his brain, because he brightened.

"Yeah, that's it! We don't really have to do that, do we? We can divide Class C into two groups. That'll take care of it, right? Ayanokouji?" he asked, lowering his voice.

It was certainly true that Class C could form two groups of ten. However, Ike's idea just wouldn't work.

"A good idea, but things aren't that simple. The rules forbid forming a group with students from just one class. As long as groups abide by the approved headcount, you are free to team up with any class you wish. But each group must have a combination of students from at least two classes. More importantly, these groups aren't selected through discussion. They must be agreed upon unanimously," said Chabashira.

What she'd just said was written plainly in the syllabus. *"Every group must consist of students from at least two or more classes."*

"So this means we have to make friends with the enemy?" Ike blurted out. It was less of a question and more of something that had just slipped out.

"Yes, exactly," replied Chabashira, looking slightly exasperated. "Of course, you could form a group that consists *almost* entirely of students from your own class. If you can get just one student from another class, you'll meet the requirements."

In other words, we could form a group of ten people—the lower limit—and then have nine of those students be from Class C. I couldn't imagine that kind of group composition would be unanimously approved when we held our school-wide discussions, though. Very few students would be willing to join a group almost entirely composed of people from another class.

However, I doubted a group like that would meet unanimous school-wide approval. Very few students would likely be willing to join a group that only had members from another class.

Also, was it better to have more people, or fewer? The same number? If the difference in numbers could create an advantage or disadvantage, a smaller group was a risk.

But we couldn't know which number would be superior without learning the test's conditions. Our luck would depend on the nature of the exam.

"I'm sure you're wondering if it's better to have more people in a group or fewer. Numbers will certainly be significant to this test, as you'll see if you turn to the section marked 'Outcomes,'" said Chabashira wryly. "I will explain it now."

Apparently, it was easy to tell we'd all been thinking the same thing.

"Excuse me, but could you please continue explaining the rules first? I want to learn about the outcomes, but before that, I'd like to know what we'll be doing as a group," asked Hirata.

"I suppose you're right. If I respond to every one of Ike's concerns, we won't get anywhere."

Ike scratched his head apologetically again.

"Each group will function like a temporary class. I say temporary, but your time together will be significant. Group members will take classes together, of course, but will also cook and clean, bathe and sleep together. You'll be sharing a variety of life experiences."

Both guys and girls let out agonized wails when they heard the words 'bathe and sleep together.'

"I really don't feel like I could live with people from

the other classes though," grumbled Ike. I understood how he felt. Though we'd cooperated with another class during the Sports Festival, that had been a brief and temporary alliance. we hadn't spent much time together. We hadn't exactly been together through thick and thin.

However, this exam was about to collapse those boundaries. Depending on how things went, some groups might even wind up with a mix of people from all four classes.

"As for outcomes, those are determined by a comprehensive test given on the last day of camp. The contents of this rather significant test are outlined on page 7 of your handouts. Give it a look."

Everyone checked that section.

Ethics
Fortitude
Discipline
Initiative

These weren't typical school subjects. This exam was going to be something removed from the course of normal classes like English or mathematics, which tested academic ability, huh? Unfortunately, I doubted the tests we were about to face would have clear answers. The four concepts outlined in the syllabus were abstract ones. I had yet to see any concrete details of how the test would be conducted.

The schedule laid out in the syllabus only proved my point. After waking up, we'd do morning assignments. Then we would gather at the dojo and engage in *zazen*, meditative discipline exercises (such as cleaning), followed by breakfast, then by various lessons in a classroom setting. After lunch, students would work on afternoon assignments, and then practice more *zazen*. Then we would have dinner, bathe, and go to bed. Quite the departure from our lifestyle up until now.

Incidentally, unlike our usual school routine, there would be additional lessons on Saturday mornings. We'd only have Sunday off.

"More details about your schedule will be announced upon arrival at camp. Right now, I cannot tell you what kind of exam you will face on the final day," added Chabashira.

So we'd need to stay on our toes and play things by ear during the special exam. Maybe the final day would test us on things like *zazen,* including fine details like posture and manners. Words like *Speech* and *Production* jumped out at me as I scanned the syllabus. They didn't feel like good signs.

"Choosing your groups will be of the utmost importance. All six groups must work together and get through the week-long school camp as a unit. No matter the reason, you cannot withdraw from your group at any time, nor can members be changed. If a student has to withdraw due to illness or injury, then their group must simply deal with their absence and operate as though that student is still part of the group."

In other words, we'd get nowhere if there was discord within the group, or if we antagonized each other. It was looking more and more like we were going to have to juggle vying with other classes with balancing the internal functioning of our own group.

Going by the schedule, lessons began tomorrow morning, which was Friday. We'd be in session until Wednesday of next week. Next Thursday, all grade levels would take the final exam.

"Once the first-year students have finished creating their groups, they will rendezvous with the second- and third-year students, who will form their own groups at the same time. In the end, we will have six final groups, each consisting of a mix of approximately thirty to forty-five first-, second-, and third-year students."

It was already tough forming a group within the same grade level, but now we were adding other grade levels on top of that. The bus got weirdly quiet.

"To put it more simply," Chabashira said, "think of groups formed of students in the same grade level as small groups. The groups formed from students in all grade levels, on the other hand, will be large groups."

Each of the six groups formed by students in the same grade level would be a small group. Then those small groups would join with the second- and third-years to ultimately form six large groups.

"Outcomes will be determined based on the average exam results of all members of the six individual large groups. The strengths and weaknesses of the other grade levels will heavily influence your results."

What concerned me here was the difference in group membership numbers. The large groups would consist of about forty people. Averaging out our results *should* help reduce inequality, but depending on how the smaller groups were formed, there might be significant differences in the number of people in the large groups.

How we chose to form those large groups was now the most important thing. If this were an academic exam, a large group with only exceptional students in it would easily win. Conversely, students who were deemed unexceptional would inevitably be excluded from the top groups, thus forced to form a lower ranked group. However, this exam couldn't be won by simply gathering the academically gifted in one place.

"I think you've probably got the gist of things now.

I'll conclude with the most important piece of information—that is to say, the results of this special exam."

Good question. What did we stand to lose?

"The members of large groups whose averaged scores take first through third place will receive both private points and class points. Large groups whose average scores place fourth or below should expect to have points deducted," explained Chabashira.

The details were, naturally, outlined in the syllabus.

Basic Rewards

1st Place: 10,000 private points. 3 class points.
2nd Place: 5000 private points. 1 class point.
3rd Place: 3000 private points.

The aforementioned rewards will be distributed to each individual student.

So if a small group of ten people included nine people from the same class, that class would be awarded twenty-seven class points as a result of the group taking first place. Of course, that was describing an ideal scenario, but it would be best to aim to have as many students as possible from our class take first place.

However, the more students from the same class there were in a group, the more points that class would have deducted if the group ranked fourth or below. And the larger the group, the trickier it would be to control everyone. The negatives at stake outweighed the relatively few positives.

4th Place: −5000 private points.
5th Place: −10,000 private points. −3 class points.
6th Place: −20,000 private points. −5 class points.

The aforementioned penalties will be deducted from each individual student.

Private points and class points couldn't fall below zero, but the deductions would remain as a cumulative deficit that would be applied against any points awarded for future exams. It was something the school had never done before. If the rewards seemed relatively small, compared to the risks, it was because there was a trick to it.

Chabashira read the next section aloud.

"Depending on the number of classes represented in a small group, rewards may be multiplied. They may also be multiplied based on the total number of people in a small group. Please relax, though. These multipliers only apply to rewards gained from placing first, second, or third. They do not apply to the point deductions for fourth place and below."

These potential reward multipliers went as follows.

If a small group comprised students from two classes,

they would receive only the base rewards. However, a small group comprising students from three classes would be rewarded with double the amount of class and private points. A group comprising students from all four classes would be rewarded with triple the amount of class and private points.

Finally, the multiplier changed depending on the number of people in a small group. A group of ten people got the base reward. A group of fifteen people got 1.5 times the reward. In the special event that a small group had only nine people, their reward would be 0.9 times the default.

In other words, if a group comprising students from all four classes obtained first place, they'd hit the 3× multiplier. If that same group *also* had the maximum number of allowed members, i.e., fifteen, they'd earn an additional 1.5× multiplier. Rounded to the nearest whole integer, this meant each member of the group would be awarded 45,000 private points and fourteen class points.

So far, this seemed like a standard special exam; tricky but interesting. But what came next changed everything.

"Also..." Chabashira said. "There is a significant penalty for the large group that comes in last place."

"A penalty...? No way."

"Yes. The penalty is expulsion."

No surprises there.

"Granted, not every member of the large group that comes in last will be expelled. If we did that, we'd be expelling nearly forty students at once. Expulsion will only apply to the small group within that large group whose average score falls below the threshold set by the school."

So overall rankings were calculated based on the average score of each large group, but when it came to expulsions, it was the average scores of the small groups that were taken into account. That was troubling.

"If a small group fails to meet that standard, then that small group's representative will be expelled."

"How do we pick the representatives?"

"You will discuss it with the members of your small group and appoint somebody. That is all."

"The hell? Who'd willingly want to be the representative knowing they might get expelled?"

I doubted there'd be many volunteers.

"There are significant benefits to being a group representative. The representative and the representative's classmates will receive double the rewards."

"Did you say double?" muttered Horikita, who had been silent until now.

"That's right. To secure the highest possible payout from this exam, you would have to form a group comprising twelve Class C students and one student from each of the remaining three classes. If you then appoint someone from Class C as your representative and take first place..."

"Wh-what do we win?" asked Yamauchi, unable to perform the calculations himself. He was practically hyperventilating.

"You'd get 1.08 million private points and 336 class points."

"Th-three hundred thirty-six?!"

If that happened, it would overturn the class rankings entirely. Even jumping all the way to A Class as a result of this exam wasn't out of the question, depending on how the other groups scored. The more risks we took, the greater the rewards—and the odds of securing the highest achievable reward weren't too low, either.

"Once the small groups have been decided, you will have until tomorrow morning to appoint your representative. In the event a group cannot choose a representative, that group will immediately be disqualified, and every single one of its members will be expelled. Of course, no group would ever be so stupid as to make such a mistake."

So the school wouldn't be picking representatives—it was solely up to us to decide who to appoint. A difficult decision, to be sure. If no one volunteered, we might wind up having to draw straws or play rock-paper-scissors...an inevitable conclusion in light of the fact we'd all be expelled otherwise, but in an already fraught situation such as this, it would put a strain on the group's unity.

"Finally, the representative who is expelled may choose one other person from within their group to share their fate. We're calling this one the solidarity rule. Think of it as going down together.'"

"H-huh?! What's with that?! That's just crazy! So, if we appointed some random dude as the representative, they could take down the leader of another class?!"

I couldn't imagine it would be that easy. Selecting a representative would involve a certain degree of screening. We probably wouldn't be picking obvious sacrificial pawns to fill the role, and if we did, it would be the group's fault. It was unlikely we'd find someone willing to both sacrifice themselves for the group's sake and take down a student from an enemy class in the process... unless, of course, we were talking about someone who'd been trapped in Class D for years and was on the verge of dropping out anyway.

But if there were students who were contemplating giving up in that way, their peers were probably aware of the fact.

"Don't worry," Chabashira said. "The representative can't just take *any* student down with them. Only students whom the school deems contributory to the group's failure can be selected for expulsion in this way. Unless you deliberately score poorly or boycott the test, you'll be fine."

Well, that was something, at least. However, I had my doubts about the representatives for this exam. This was unlike any previous situation we'd been in—particularly the fact that this time, the exam was the same for all grade levels. The other classes were probably receiving the exact same instructions right now.

In other words, many different strategies were currently in the process of being formed. This wasn't just a fight between the first-years. The second-years were battling other second-years and third-years other third-years.

I sent off a text message to a certain individual, hoping to clear a few things up. I wanted to know if the student council was somehow involved in creating this special exam.

"One more important detail. If a student is expelled, that student's class will be penalized accordingly. The specifics of the penalty change depending on the exam. In the case of this test, one hundred points will be deducted from the class. If the class has insufficient class points to pay off the penalty, they will be in debt. Until that debt is paid off, their total will remain at zero."

The benefits were enormous, but the negatives were

just as vast. The promise of doubling your points by being a group representative was tantalizing, but it came with the risk of being expelled. No one would willingly volunteer for such a role unless they were confident in the abilities of their small group. Nor, however, would they want the spoils of the representative's victory to go to another class.

Then there was the solidarity rule, which was clearly designed to leave you at an impasse.

"That concludes my explanation. I will now open the floor for questions."

Hirata immediately raised his hand.

"If someone were to be expelled...would there be any way to help that person, like a lifeline?" he asked.

"If you're expelled, you're expelled. Nothin' ya can do 'bout it," replied Sudou.

Hirata rejected that outright. "That can't be true. You were almost expelled once, Sudou-kun, but were saved thanks to Horikita-san's quick thinking. It would be strange if there was nothing we could do."

Chabashira smiled.

"That's correct. You can buy a Revocation of Expulsion using private points as a last resort. Naturally, the price will be high. The Revocation of Expulsion costs twenty million private points *and* an additional three hundred class points. This lifeline will only prevent a student's expulsion. It won't cancel out the penalties suffered by the class as a result of that expulsion. Of course, if you don't have the points to pay for the lifeline, then that option is unavailable."

An exorbitant price. It meant a minimum of four hundred class points would be required to save a student on the brink of expulsion, which made it a lifeline we were unlikely to extend. The whole class would have to pay a great toll to save one person.

"Regarding the twenty million points you mentioned, can the entire class pitch in?" asked Hirata, who was clearly considering a future where we might use the lifeline.

"Yes, everyone may pitch in. But this is completely irrelevant, since you have only a few points available."

With that, Chabashira was done reviewing the materials.

"There isn't much time left before we reach our destination. You are free to use the remaining time however you like. Right before we arrive, I will re-collect the handout. Also, the use of phones will be forbidden for a week. I will be collecting those shortly. Other than that, you are free to bring daily necessities or playthings along with you, but not food. Perishables must be consumed before we arrive, or you'll have to throw them away before you get off the bus. That's all."

Students who hadn't reacted to the dangers of the special exam now let out agonized wails at that last comment. We'd already gone through this on the uninhabited island, but I supposed it was painful to have your phone confiscated for a whole week.

"I have a question!" Ike raised his hand energetically. "You said that guys and girls would be separate, but, like, exactly how spread out are we gonna be?"

Chabashira wore a wry smile. "There are two buildings at the camp. The boys will use the main building, and the girls will take the other. The buildings are next to one another, but you'll be living apart from each other for a week. You will not be allowed to go outside during recess or after school without permission either."

"So we won't be able to talk to each other?"

"No, boys and girls will take meals together in the cafeteria in the main building for one hour a day. The school issues no directives to students during that time period. You can do as you please then. Understand?"

"Yes!" Ike rejoiced, probably happy he'd be able to talk to girls.

I sat up slightly and glanced at Shinohara, who was sitting nearby. While she looked slightly exasperated, her face brightened at Ike's words. Maybe their Christmas dinner had gone well.

"If there are no further questions, that'll be all," said Chabashira, probably anticipating a lot of silly questions coming her way.

"Sensei. May I borrow your microphone?" asked Hirata.

"Of course." Chabashira handed it over and returned to her seat. Hirata took her place at the front of the bus.

"Based on what sensei said, we're running out of time. Still, I'd like to try to hear everyone's opinions. How can we get through this exam? What kind of groups should we shoot for?"

"Wouldn't it be best if we tried to get as many of our classmates in as possible? Pick twelve toppers and then get one person from every other class. That'd be perfect," said Sudou.

"That would be ideal, but I doubt three students from other classes would want to join that group. They'd naturally be on their guard."

It would be obvious that such a group wanted to win badly. I couldn't imagine single students from each of the other classes being willing to join them. Besides, if such a group ranked poorly, the damage to the class would be considerable.

"Hey, if all the smart people get in one group, then the rest of us don't stand a chance," said Yamauchi. Apparently, he still hadn't figured out that this wasn't about academics. "I mean, we really wanna get some private points ourselves."

His complaints were understandable. This issue had come up during the exam on the cruise ship too. The large group who ranked first would earn private points, but the students in the bottom groups gained nothing. In fact, they would lose a great deal. Given that, most people obviously wanted to bet on the winning horse by joining a large group that was likely to win.

"If everyone here agrees, I'd like to propose an even distribution," Hirata said. "We don't know which group will come out on top. If any of us gain private points from this exam, we'll distribute those points evenly across the class. That should be fine, since point transfers are allowed."

And if we got hit with a deduction, it wouldn't be so bad, since everyone would be sharing the load.

"Ah, I see. That's okay."

Of course, the more exceptional students would complain about this, but considering what was at stake, a consensus seemed likely.

"Heh."

After hearing Hirata's proposal, Chabashira chuckled, facing away from him.

"I didn't tell you this because you didn't ask, but as a reward for your promotion to Class C, I will give you one bit of helpful advice."

Advice?

Hirata looked cautious, not ready to accept this reward at face value.

"When the rules don't forbid it, you're certainly free to transfer points. Be it in the middle of an exam or in the course of your daily life—you can transfer points as much as you please, as long as you don't break any rules in the process. However, private points are not pocket money. You'd do well to remember that."

"Are you saying we could, like, transfer to any class we wanted if we accumulated like twenty million points? Or is this about the lifeline?"

"I'm saying there are many different ways of using private points. Having as little as one point can help you in a time of need. Getting along and supporting each other isn't always going to be the correct answer, you understand? For example, let's say Ike made a mistake that would lead to him being expelled unless a million private points were paid right away—and the school disallowed transferring points in that instance. Ike would have to produce the million points himself or be expelled. What then? If you divide your points up equally, you might end up doing something you can't take back."

Ike gulped loudly when he heard himself used as an example.

"You can't count on other students to save you, because every single one of them might find themselves in need the next moment. The only one who can protect you is you, yourself," said Chabashira. "People who work hard are rewarded. That much is obvious. Once you enter the real world, it's exceedingly unlikely you'll find people who'd gladly share their salary and bonuses with friends."

Perhaps we should be grateful for the advice...but this was just going to make it harder to unite the class. I didn't doubt everything she was saying was true; I couldn't imagine any teacher at this school would stir up trouble just because there was no precedent for something. Chabashira always played by the rules.

That said, there was more to this conversation.

I was sure there had been prior instances of individuals saving up private points. But conversely, I was equally sure there had been incidents where students were saved because their classmates had accumulated a great many points. How did I know this? Well, from personal experience. In the past, Horikita and I worked out a solution to provide Sudou with points when it seemed he was about to be expelled. That then set a precedent.

Ultimately, sharing points evenly among ourselves could be seen as a preventative measure to be deployed in unforeseen situations. Having individual students hold onto a large number of points raised the risk of that person embezzling those points or betraying the class.

Chabashira had just said something that disrupted her own class's chances at cohesion. I couldn't reject the possibility that it was just school policy, of course, but...

"Well, shall we put it to a majority vote? I'd like to at least hear what everyone is thinking. Can the people who want to split the rewards please raise your hands? It's okay if you change your mind later," said Hirata. He lifted his hand at once.

Only a few hands went up. Most of my classmates looked worried. Coming together as a class was import-ant, sure, but when push came to shove, you had to have a way to protect yourself. Most students probably had only somewhere between ten thousand to a hundred thousand private points. Given that, it was no wonder many wanted to keep those points as a safety net.

Students who lacked confidence in their own abilities, on the other hand, were more likely to want points to be shared across the class. There were a few more such students than I'd expected, but in the end, less than half the class raised their hands.

"Thank you."

The majority was against point splitting. Hirata's motion had failed.

"Was my advice unnecessary, Hirata?" Chabashira asked.

"No, I'm thankful for it. It's valuable information at this stage."

My phone vibrated. Thinking the certain individual whom I'd messaged might have replied, I took my phone out of my pocket—but it was his little sister, Horikita, who'd texted me. Naturally, it was about the special exam.

"Do you have any ideas?" she wrote. Jeez, always trying to make me do things.

"None," I replied. After thinking it over, I sent another message. *"Guys and girls are going to be separated in this exam. I can't help with anything. Do your best."*

My attempt to offer her some encouragement. I was sure Horikita had a lot she wanted to say in return, but I didn't want to listen. I closed the text thread and checked on another of my group chats: that of the Ayanokouji Group (named after myself, but not in a boastful way).

Keisei, Akito, and even Airi and Haruka all happily discussed the exam. I read through their texts, closed the chat without adding any comments, and resumed listening to Hirata.

"We don't have enough time to come up with a strategy," he was saying. "If the boys and girls are going to be separated, sending advice to each other will get tricky."

"No way..." The girls looked understandably uneasy at the prospect of being unable to turn to Hirata, who held the class together and had always been a guy they could rely on.

"Since the boys won't be able to lend a hand, I think the girls should decide on a leader right now. Will you accept the role, Horikita-san?"

Hirata had probably been chewing over this since Chabashira began to explain the exam. He'd singled out Horikita because she was the only one capable of handling the role.

"Very well. If anyone's having difficulties, feel free to approach me at any time. I don't mind," replied Horikita. She showed no signs of displeasure, but, even though she was gradually becoming more of a person our classmates could depend on, she didn't warrant anywhere near the level of trust that Hirata did. Of course, being Horikita, she was surely aware of that.

"However, I'm sure quite a few of the other girls will find me lacking," she continued. "I don't like to say this of myself, but I have a somewhat abrasive personality."

Yeah, that really wasn't something anyone would want to admit.

"Which is why I'd like Kushida-san to assist me. What do you think?" said Horikita, directing this to Kushida, who sat near the front of the bus.

"W-will I even be useful?" asked Kushida.

"Of course. Everyone in our class trusts you."

"Um… Well, okay. If you'd like, I'll help."

"Thank you. In the event someone finds it difficult to speak directly with me, you can do so via Kushida-san. I don't mind. I will respond to any issue, no matter how trivial."

While Kushida's trustworthiness was a matter of some concern, this strategy was unquestionably the best we had right now. The exam rules made it fairly difficult for guys and girls to meddle in each other's affairs. Despite being held in the same general facility, our classes and tests would take place in separate locations. The guys would have no opportunity to participate in any of the battles being fought on the girls' side. With our phones being confiscated to boot, our only opportunity for contact would be the one hour we had for dinner.

That being said, it was vital we be able to gather as much information as possible. I was going to need a gofer to funnel information to me from the girls. Kushida worried me. This left Horikita or Kei as options, and the former had a lot on her plate right now. I also had to consider the fact that she tended to read too much into my intentions and take unnecessary actions.

More importantly, if she was going to be fielding consultation pleas from the other girls, she probably wouldn't have energy to spare for much else. I supposed I'd have to use Kei after all, though I couldn't force her to survey the entire group by herself.

I sent the bare minimum of necessary information over to Kei's phone. She immediately replied with a blank message to confirm receipt. Given we'd just learned that the unique nature of this test would force the guys and girls to do battle separately for a while, she must have assumed I'd be contacting her.

Kei probably wanted some advice herself right now. Considering the rules of this exam, particularly the ones about the representatives and their ability to take someone down with them, it wasn't outside the realm of possibility that Kei might wind up as a sacrificial pawn. I couldn't say she was doing well at the moment, whether in terms of her test scores or her behavior in class.

That was why I was going to teach her a few tricks to protect herself. They weren't things that every student could pull off, but they could keep you safer, if only slightly so.

As for me, I couldn't really care less about the special exam. I had no intention of executing any winning strategies. All I wanted was to make it through safely and without incident.

This didn't mean I wouldn't be making any moves at all—like what I'd just done by giving Kei advice. In a worst-case scenario, this special exam could lead to several students getting expelled from C Class. I couldn't protect the entire class by myself. I had to narrow down the list of people I wanted to safeguard.

Besides myself, I wanted to protect Kei, who'd become a staunch ally, and Hirata. Considering my involvement with the student council, I needed to ensure that Horikita stuck around, too. Then there were my friends: Keisei, Akito, Haruka, and Airi. They couldn't be my top priority, but as their friend, I certainly hoped they wouldn't be expelled.

Finally, given this rare opportunity for grade levels to intermingle, I should keep an eye on Nagumo's movements. Any other minor skirmishes that occurred around me were beneath my notice.

2.1

THE BUS GOT OFF the highway and began to drive up the paved mountain road. I wondered why our school outings always took place in nature, like this location or the ocean.

At any rate, a new special exam was about to begin. Given they were confiscating our phones, this was certainly going to be that annoying kind of test where you had to gather information either on your own or by using your connections. And, since more information would be leaked the more carelessly you acted, prudence and discretion would be vital.

"I'm not cut out for this..." I muttered, letting my honest thoughts slip forth.

No matter how many special exams we went through,

I just couldn't get used to them. I'd so rarely had to cooperate with other people before.

"We will arrive shortly," Chabashira said. "Once there, you will form your groups. Then, as soon as room assignments have been completed, you will have lunch, followed by free time in the afternoon."

"That means... Yay! We don't have to study!" Ike beamed at me.

True, but this wasn't vacation. It was a school day. Even taking the travel time into account, it was odd that they were letting us off the hook this afternoon—it felt almost like a normal field trip, which couldn't be right.

The bus pulled into the stop and slowed to a halt.

"When your name is called, hand over your phone and get off the bus. Ayanokouji. Ike—"

Chabashira started with the boys, calling our names in syllabary order. I turned my phone off and put it in a plastic box that sat next to our teacher. As I disembarked from the bus, an unfamiliar teacher approached, instructing us to wait a short distance away from the bus.

"Dude, it's cold!" shouted Ike, hugging himself tightly. Probably because we were in the mountains. It was certainly colder here than at school.

However, the sight before us made us forget the cold for a moment.

"Whoa. What *is* this place? This seems a lot for a 'school camp'..."

Enormous grounds spread out before us, with some *extremely* old-fashioned school buildings visible in the distance. Our home for the next week. They were huge, probably because they had to accommodate the students of all three grade levels.

It felt similar to the test on the uninhabited island. As with that test, I really didn't have much experience living out in the wilds like this. People like Ike, who had been a boy scout, were going to be useful here. So would those like Sudou, with their physical strength.

The girls filed off the bus next. It seemed like Horikita wanted to come talk to me, but unfortunately, we were already being queued up into separate lines. The boys and girls each headed for our respective school buildings, with the boys being directed to the larger one, referred to as the main building. Once inside, I found my nostrils tickled by the nostalgic scent of the wood-paneled interior.

"This really is a traditional wooden school building, isn't it? It's old, but still beautiful. It must be exceptionally well maintained," said Hirata. Everyone else agreed.

Along the way, we saw what appeared to be a classroom. There was no air conditioning, only a single stove placed in the center of the room. We'd most likely be having classes from tomorrow in rooms like that.

Finally, we arrived at what seemed like a gymnasium. The guys from Class A and Class B, who were already there, looked over our way. The Class D students showed up right after us, so the second- and third-year students were probably on their way in next.

We were ordered to form a line and await further instruction. Classes A and B looked calm and didn't chat amongst themselves. They'd probably already finished strategizing on the bus, huh?

• •

BOYS FROM EVERY grade level assembled inside the gymnasium. The bashful first-year students clumped together to wait in silence, and soon after, a teacher from one of the senior classes took to the stage, microphone in hand.

"I'm going to assume you all understand the contents of the exam after the explanation you were given on the bus ride," he addressed us. "Each grade level will now hold internal discussions and form into six small groups. The large groups will be formed at 8:00 p.m. today. That is all. As a reminder, the school will play no part in the formation of these groups, whether large or small. Nor will school officials act as mediators."

Okay, then. I wondered what the other classes' strategies were? They should have some plans in place already, but...we'd see how it went.

Each grade level—first-, second-, and third-years—distanced themselves from one another, and the discussions began. I was curious about what the seniors were doing, but it was hard to make out any details from here.

As I attempted to observe them, though, there was already movement taking place within the first-year classes. I'd thought we'd try to feel each other out a little longer, but Class A got straight to work, forming one large group. A pretty attention-grabbing move, given the stalemate we were in.

There were twenty boys in first-year Class A. Fourteen of them formed up into a single group, then made the following declaration to the people in Class B and below.

"As you can see, we in Class A intend to form a single group in this fashion. We have fourteen people at present and need one more person to meet the requirements. We are looking for someone to join us."

The person who said this was a Class A student named Matoba. I saw Katsuragi among the fourteen boys in the group, but if Matoba was the leader, did that mean Katsuragi wasn't the representative either? At any rate, this made it clear that Class A's strategy was to form a group made up of as many of their own people as possible.

"Hey, hey! What the hell are you selfish punks doing? It ain't fair if you're the only ones who go and do something like that," said Sudou, glaring angrily at Class A.

"Is it selfish? Our group would comprise students representing only two classes. Even if we take first place, our modifier will be low. I don't think this is a greedy proposal at all."

"W-well, sure. But it's unfair that there's fourteen of ya."

"On the contrary, it's very fair. Since the remaining three classes can create three groups of fifteen people each, you can all make groups similar to ours. Right?"

"Uh, I guess?" said Sudou, not quite understanding. He looked to Hirata for help.

"That is correct, yes," said Hirata.

"Then this discussion is pointless. By the way, we've agreed that the six remaining boys from Class A will happily join whatever groups you make, no matter their makeup," said Matoba, smiling broadly. He turned to Class B's Kanzaki and Shibata as well.

"Um... Well, I guess this isn't really a bad deal at all. What do you think, Kanzaki?"

"Sorry, I need more time to answer that," Kanzaki said.

"I can't imagine that Class A students would go so far as to deliberately drag the other classes down, but I suppose it's best to be cautious..."

Class A was pushing everyone to come to a decision right away, but Kanzaki didn't seem inclined to rush. In response to his stalling, Matoba came back with a strongly worded statement. "You have five minutes. Please make your decision by then."

"A time limit? We've only just begun to discuss this. Class A gave us an opinion, not an order—you don't get to make an unilateral decision here. A five-minute window is absurd."

Despite Class A's claim that going along with their proposal meant each class could make their own group of fourteen people, it would be a lie to say that this was fair for all classes. If you thought about it, Class A was the only class that could afford not to care about a low reward modifier. They were currently ranked first and leading in points.

"I suppose it wouldn't be fair of us to make this decision solely by ourselves," Matoba said. "But you misunderstand. We're not saying we won't negotiate after the five minutes are up. We're just offering special terms for someone within that five minutes."

"Special terms?"

Matoba continued to control the conversation, precisely because the other classes had yet to solidify what they wanted. This was certainly close to what you'd call a preemptive strike.

"Class A is going to form one group of fourteen people, meaning we require one student from another class. Setting aside the merits of this strategy, it's certainly true that we're selfishly pushing this idea on you. As such, the single person whom we will welcome into our group will receive special treatment," he explained eloquently.

This had to be the strategy they'd come up with on the bus.

"The student who joins our group will bear no risk whatsoever. Katsuragi-kun will act as the group's representative, and in the unlikely event that we place last, he will take full responsibility. No one will be dragged down via the solidarity rule. Of course, this only applies so long as the special entrant doesn't intentionally lower our scores or hurt our friends. If your exam scores are genuinely poor despite your best efforts, that's fine."

So these were the special terms, huh?

"Are you serious...?"

The proposal had its merits. Gathering skilled team members in one place to create a group with a high point modifier might be necessary to advance a class, but it was those skilled people—the people at the very heart of the class—who bore the risks of such a strategy going sour. From the perspective of an average student, who grappled with fears of expulsion, Matoba's proposed system of special treatment wasn't a bad idea at all. It would guarantee they made it safely through this special exam.

Still, why wasn't Katsuragi the one suggesting this? Was this the fallout of him losing status within the class?

"We intend to take first place, meaning there is a strong possibility that our special entrant will be rewarded with private points. Aren't many of you nervous about this special exam?" asked Matoba, looking around. His words clearly resonated with the less secure students. "However, if you cannot decide within the five-minute window, the special offer expires. In the unlikely event that our class does receive a penalty, we will not hesitate to drag that student down with us."

"It's an interesting proposal. But after the five minutes have passed, the value of joining your group plummets significantly. No one wants to join a team with such a high risk of taking them down with it," said Kanzaki.

"Yeah, that's right. Who'd be crazy enough to do that?" said a student who'd been briefly charmed by the idea of the special terms.

"I don't mind what you think. But these are our terms," said Matoba, taking a step back. His group moved with him, signaling the end of the discussion.

"I think we're better off ignoring them. Once five minutes have passed, no one will want to join their group. They'll be back," said Kanzaki.

"Suppose so," said Shibata.

Having said that, they moved calmly away. I didn't see Kaneda and the other newly demoted Class D students making any strange movements either.

Hirata, however, seemed to be the sole person who felt differently about Class A's proposal. He approached Keisei, Akito, and me, asking, "What do you think?" in a low voice.

"About their strategy?" replied Keisei, taking the lead in the conversation.

"Yeah. Surprisingly enough, I don't think it's a bad deal. It is absolutely essential that everyone in Class C makes it through. We've only just been promoted, and I don't want any of my classmates to be expelled. If a student who's nervous about this exam joins Class A's group, they should be able to rest easy," said Hirata.

As a defensive strategy, Class A's proposal had its merits.

"Of course, it remains to be seen whether Class A will keep their promise of special treatment. If they wind up taking last place, they might use the solidarity rule to take someone down with them, after all," he added.

Hirata's anxieties were understandable. Verbal agreements *were* binding in nature, but even if we confronted Class A about it in the wake of a betrayal, they could trap us in endless arguments that went nowhere. If they feigned ignorance, then things would get complicated. After all, their promise hinged on no one intentionally sabotaging the group. If a student's exam scores were low, it would be difficult to prove whether or not it was intentional.

Still, we couldn't exactly get it in writing; there weren't any pens or paper at hand. The teachers had been ordered not to help, so asking them to bear witness to a verbal promise would probably be useless too.

That being said, Matoba's words had piqued the interest of all of the first-year students. He stood to gain nothing by going back on his words. It might be okay to trust Class A on this.

"...It might be possible to have them protect one person," I stated, joining Hirata and Keisei's conversation.

"Yeah. If we make a move now, that just leaves the question of what B and D decide..."

Accepting the offer would be seen as siding with Class A, who had opted for a heavy-handed approach. Even though we only had a tiny window, Hirata seemed to want to think this over until the last possible second.

Roughly three minutes had passed since Class A's sudden proposal. We didn't know whether they were dutifully counting every second, but Matoba and the others seemed to be leisurely standing by.

Maybe they were expecting someone to raise their hand. Or maybe they were thinking up another strategy. We watched them carefully for the remaining two minutes, waiting for them to make their move—though what they would do, of course, depended on the leaders of classes B and below.

"Kanzaki-shi. I have a proposal. Would you care to hear it?" said Kaneda.

Rather than whisper, he raised his voice boldly so that everyone could hear, beckoning Hirata to join them too.

"I've determined that this is an opportunity we should seize," he said. "Thanks to Class A forming up like this, even if their group does happen to win in this exam, they only get a point modifier for representing two classes. Moreover, if we accept their conditions, we can assign the remaining Class A students as we see fit. We could configure the remaining groups to include students from all four classes, meaning the higher those groups ranked, the greater the likelihood of their members closing the gap between their class and Class A. Correct?"

"That's only if we can rank higher than them, though."

I didn't know what the exact scores were, but during the Paper Shuffle, Class A had destroyed Class B. In a test of academic skill, this could end badly.

"It's certainly risky. However, this isn't merely a question of academics. What do you think? I say we try to overthrow Class A here and now," said Kaneda.

In other words, have B, C, and D cooperate to lay siege against Class A here.

"Letting Class A have a group of fourteen of their people is a small price to pay, compared to the point multiplier for representing all four classes in a single group. With their offer of special treatment on top of that, it should work out perfectly."

"That's right. I like Kaneda-kun's strategy," said Hirata. Kanzaki, more cautious, continued to ruminate on the benefits of having people from all four classes in a single group.

"But who's going to join Class A's main group?" he said. "I doubt any Class B students want to team up with them. Myself included."

Even if the special entrant would be protected from expulsion, he'd be spending the week in a group made up only of Class A students. It was safe to say it wouldn't be the most comfortable time.

"Let's ask students from Classes B and D. Would anyone like to step forward?" said Hirata.

We looked at each other. But no one raised their hand.

"Then I'd like to ask Class C. Would anyone like to step forward?" asked Hirata, directing the question to our own class this time. But he got the same reaction.

Some were likely considering the offer because of the special quota but also anxious about having everyone's eyes on them. Not to mention being behind enemy lines for a week.

"This is just my opinion," said Hirata, "but I think Class A will keep their word."

"How can you know that?"

"Because they're Class A, I suppose. If they do force a lower-ranking student into expulsion despite their promise, no one will ever trust them enough to make a deal with them again. We're only in the third semester of our first year. To lose credibility now would be a significant setback."

Hirata's words made sense. If this were a final, decisive battle, Class A might act without care for their reputation. But they still had over two years to go. If they were seen to keep their word here, they could continue to use similar methods in the exams to come. Hirata was saying they wouldn't do anything too reckless just yet.

"Not to praise an enemy, but this is Class A. Their grades are simply better than ours. I doubt they'll come last or drop below the average. Your safety would be guaranteed."

Ike and the others could understand that temptation well.

"Fortunately, there don't appear to be any Class B or D candidates. I'd like to choose someone from Class C to join A's group. Even if they do win, our class would benefit, and someone would avoid the chance of expulsion. How does that sound?" said Hirata.

He specifically directed his gaze to Ike and Yamauchi, no doubt wanting to protect students who were anxious about their abilities. He made sure to confirm the truth of what he was saying with Matoba too.

"Even if the special entrant scores below the group's average, do you promise you won't seek to punish them?" he asked Matoba.

"Of course. We ask nothing of that student. If they uphold the conditions I outlined earlier, they have my word."

"I suppose I'll do it," muttered Ike. Upon hearing that, Yamauchi said the same.

"I think I would like to volunteer myself as well," added the Professor, bringing us to three candidates.

"To keep things fair, how about we settle this with rock-paper-scissors? The winner joins the group," suggested Hirata. They did just that, with Yamauchi emerging victorious, making him the person chosen to join Class A's main group. And thus, the first group was formed. They reported to Mashima-sensei, leaving the six remaining Class A students behind.

"Now we can form the remaining groups however we wish. I suppose we could do as Class A suggested and form three groups of fourteen people from the same class. And, just like Class A, we could pledge not to invoke the solidarity rule against the one person from another class. Personally, however, I would prefer we do as I had suggested earlier and blend all four classes together."

"That's right. Now that we're goin' with Class A's plan, I think we should blend 'em."

"No objections here. What do you say, Class C?"

Kanzaki and Kaneda's strategy was one designed to secure the highest point multiplier.

"If we're aiming to win, this is what we need to do. No argument from me."

"Wait a minute, Hirata. Is this really okay? Like, I don't wanna join a group with someone like Ishizaki in it," interrupted Sudou.

It wasn't just Sudou either. Keisei and other Class C students felt similarly, and grumbled complaints could be heard from a number of Class B and D students too. Having students from all four classes got you a high multiplier, but it also courted conflict. If students who fought like cats and dogs got stuck in the same group, it might even affect scores.

"I understand. I don't think this is something we can decide immediately. What works for Class A may not work for us."

Given how satisfied the Class A students looked, they'd probably agreed to split the rewards equally among all their classmates. They might even have promised to give the six students excluded from their main group a greater share of the rewards to offset the greater risks they faced. They could afford to do so precisely because they were Class A and in a relatively safe position.

"Why don't we form hypothetical groups for the time being? If anyone objects, we can stop and start over."

"Sounds good. Trying to feel things out wastes precious time and won't get us to a consensus, and Class A's already moved onto the next step."

Arguing back and forth would get us nowhere. The other students must have been leaving matters to their respective leaders, because there were almost no dissenting opinions.

"No objections here," said Kaneda, accepting the offer without any resistance. We began to form groups smoothly and efficiently. Even though no one had spoken up, though, many students still wore skeptical looks on their faces.

Ryuuen, not Kaneda, had been Class D's original leader. Everyone here was aware of that. But Ryuuen wasn't participating in the group discussion at all. In fact, he was keeping his distance from everyone and didn't even look like he was paying attention. Now that the third semester was underway, it was common knowledge that he'd vacated his position of authority a while ago. Among the students who didn't know the specific details behind his fall, there were several who suspected that the whole thing was a charade.

"I'd like to ask you something. Did Ryuuen tell you to do this?" asked Shibata, voicing the question Hirata and even Kanzaki didn't dare to.

Kaneda removed his glasses and blew dust off the lenses. "No. This was my idea. His opinions are irrelevant. And even if he and I were collaborating behind the scenes, I'm the one talking to you right now. Any problem with that?"

His expression turned somewhat grim.

"I just wanted to make sure. Sorry if I offended you," Shibata apologized.

"You didn't. Now let's continue with our discussion. We don't have the time for chit-chat."

Designing these groups was a tricky task. Each group would have to work as a team, while their individual members tried to avoid expulsion and assist their class at the same time. It might sound easy, but it wasn't. The process of group formation involved securing capable players while trying not to get stuck with any duds.

We needed to make sure the students who were likely to drag the rest down wound up in someone else's group. Hirata, Kanzaki, and Kaneda chose to act as representatives for their respective groups, shelving the matter of the remaining small groups for now.

Immediate volunteers from Class C flocked to Hirata. Having a classmate as your group representative meant you were probably safe from being dragged down with them via the solidarity rule, and you already knew them well to boot. A good way to minimize interference from other classes. People clustered in this fashion, with Class B showing similar trends. Their group members were decided faster than I could have imagined.

Class D was the last to form up, and they did so slowly. I probably wasn't the only one keeping my eye on them. Prominent students like Kanzaki and Shibata were observing them, of course, but so were many others, all curious to know exactly how Ryuuen Kakeru fit into the Class D puzzle right now.

No one trusted Class D at all. Understandable, given how many times Ryuuen Kakeru had tried to entrap us.

"What are you going to do, Kiyotaka?" Keisei and Akito came over to check in with me.

"What about you?" I asked, batting the question back at them while donning a conflicted expression face.

"I'm thinking of sticking with Keisei. I mean, using my head really isn't my strong suit."

"...A group composed mainly of C Class students is appealing. It's just, well, to be honest...I'm not really satisfied with Hirata's way of doing things."

"Meaning?" asked Akito, not understanding what Keisei was getting at.

"Hirata focuses on protecting his comrades, rather than winning. That's not a bad thing, but it doesn't advance us as a class. Also, Ike, Onizuka, and Sotomura are hoping to join Hirata's group. How they perform will depend on the nature of the upcoming tests, of course. They might even score better than me. But it's far more likely that they won't, given what this exam is shaping up to be like."

"Well, that's true..."

"Class A isn't an unruly mob. Even if Yamauchi drags them down, it's doubtful Hirata's group could win against them. The only thing we accomplish under his strategy is avoiding being taken out by the solidarity rule. Given that, I think that I'd rather be the minority in another group. We should aim for victory, using an elite few."

"If this whole thing comes down to average scores, that's a solid approach, I suppose."

There were eighty boys in the first year, twenty in each respective class. If we divided them up, here's how the four main groups would look:

GROUP A (14 A, 1 C) = 15 people

GROUP B (12 B, 1 A, 1 C, 1 D) = 15 people

GROUP C (12 C, 1 A, 1 B, 1 D) = 15 people

GROUP D (12 D, 1 A, 1 C, 1 B) = 15 people

That left twenty people (three from Class A, six from B, five from C, six from D) who would probably have to form two groups. However, while the majority of students were doing as their class leaders directed, some didn't seem inclined to cooperate. One such student was unmistakably Class D's Ryuuen Kakeru, who had avoided interacting with anyone, standing around alone as if he had no interest in participating in this exam in the first place.

Despite being alone, it didn't look like he was wallowing in loneliness, or anything. If anything, he looked like he was proudly waiting out his solitude. Either way, one of the remaining groups was going to have to take him in.

There was only one student I could imagine doing such a thing in a situation where even Ishizaki, Ryuuen's classmate, wouldn't talk to him.

"Ryuuen-kun. Would you care to join our team?"

Of course, it was Hirata.

I could understand why someone like Ryuuen, who'd halfway retired from inter-class competition, would find a mandatory-collaboration exam like this one annoying. That said, he probably wouldn't imprudently defy the school's will either.

"Wait, Hirata! Taking Ryuuen? That isn't funny!"

Everyone who'd joined Hirata's group resisted. Who'd want to work alongside the ultimate ticking time bomb? Ryuuen was the single most unnecessary element of a strategy to climb to Class A. The students understood this—but at the same time, they had doubts rising within them.

Doubts, that is, about the scenario where they graduated "from a class other than A."

Failing to graduate in Class A meant they would never benefit from this school's too-good-to-be-true guarantee of getting you into any institution or career you wanted. What was even the point of graduating if you couldn't do it in Class A?

That question haunted everyone at this school. It was the same kind of mingled unease you got when good news and bad news reached you at the same time. Without Class A, you'd be labeled an underperformer. Universities or workplaces might outright refuse to admit or hire those who didn't have what it took.

Of course, there were undoubtedly many who held graduates of the Advanced Nurturing High School in high regard. Spending three long, hard years in the pure meritocracy of a government-sponsored school had its own value. Graduating from this school at all was still a substantial achievement, as long as you didn't get your hopes up too high.

As for the second-year students, Nagumo was already top dog of Class A, far ahead of Class B and below. With a year left to go, other classes could still turn things around, but it was an uphill battle. The third-year students had it tough, too. While their situation certainly wasn't as one-sided as the second-years, I had heard that Class A, where Horikita's brother was placed, had never once surrendered its lead and was still going strong.

At this point, there was almost no chance for the second- and third-years in Class D to make any kind of comeback, barring some kind of miracle... Maybe if this were one of those quiz shows where you could shoot to first place simply by getting the crucial final question right. But I doubted that would happen here.

Putting aside the first-year students who hadn't yet grasped the bigger picture, everyone was likely terrified of expulsion. I couldn't imagine a university or employer welcoming an expelled student with open arms.

The systems in place for this exam, like the solidarity rule, were deterrents at best.

The systems in place in this exam, like the representative being able to drag someone down with them, was at most a deterrent. It was a rule created to ensure that students wouldn't be getting forcefully expelled. However, being vigilant was still important. There was still a possibility that there was a student out there who didn't mind getting expelled, and in the off chance that a representative gets expelled, they probably wouldn't hesitate to bring someone else down with them.

This meant everyone would be wise to score higher than their representative, even if only by one point, to escape the solidarity rule. Also, it was important not to incur the representative's wrath.

"Oh, ho, ain't you a big shot, Hirata, takin' me in. But it doesn't look like people are on board," said Ryuuen.

That's right. They wouldn't agree, and the group wouldn't form unless Hirata managed to talk them into it.

"Hey, Keisei. Wouldn't being part of an elite crew be

pretty risky?" muttered Akito, looking at the remaining members.

"Yeah, maybe more than I thought."

Keisei let out an exasperated sigh. Aside from me, the remaining five Class C students were Keisei, Akito, the Professor, Onizuka, and Kouenji. The Professor and Onizuka had wanted to join Hirata's group, but that group was full up. As for Kouenji, he did his own thing, so to speak. He didn't participate in any discussion.

We could argue that we'd like those five to all stick together, but then we'd have two groups of ten remaining, meaning the other classes wouldn't be able to make the same move. On top of that, since there were practically no students left who would proactively step up and take on the role of representative, students' movements became rigid, as if time had come to a halt.

"As long as I'm not in a group with Ryuuen, I'm good," said a Class B student.

"I'd also like to avoid Ryuuen," said Keisei.

Everyone was on team Not Ryuuen, probably because they had no idea what he might do next. Even his old allies, like Ishizaki, kept their distance. Shiina Hiyori, who hadn't been involved in that rooftop scuffle, might have supported Ryuuen, but she wasn't here.

"This isn't going to be easy."

"The best plan would be to put him with the Class D group."

"That would be great, sure, but we're in a bit of a bind right now."

"I heard they had a falling out. But I don't have enough evidence to know if that's true."

It was understandable that Kanzaki—no, that everyone here—would have doubts. They probably saw this whole situation as Class D intentionally cutting Ryuuen loose in the hopes he'd sabotage someone else.

"Kanzaki-kun," Hirata said. "If Ryuuen-kun really is having trouble, I think that we should do something about it."

"By 'do something about it,' you mean Classes B and C should help him. Is that it?"

"Yes."

"Even if it helps out Class D, two other classes would be hurt in the process. If you weigh the risks, it's not a good idea."

Kanzaki was right. If including Ryuuen meant taking a risk, then that risk should be shouldered by his own class. Kaneda and Ishizaki might not like the situation, but they had no right to saddle another class with Ryuuen, and we didn't need to take responsibility for their problems.

Mind you, if we'd been competing in pairs, Hirata would probably have paired up with Ryuuen in the blink of an eye. But this was a group test. One person's good-will couldn't carry the day, as evinced by the silence that followed.

It seemed forming groups was going to take longer than expected. The paranoia and suspicion emerging from the three groups that had formed right off the bat as a result of excluding Ryuuen didn't help.

2.3

. . . .

"ALLOW ME to suggest something. The problem we're facing right now is Ryuuen. We're fighting over which group to put him in, right? In that case, I'd be willing to act as a group's representative in exchange for that group taking Ryuuen," said Akito, who had been carefully observing the situation next to me.

Of course, declaring that he would accept Ryuuen when no one else wanted to instantly raised people's suspicions.

"What are you plotting?"

"It's simple. In return, I want the lion's share of the reward for first place."

I didn't think people would resist the idea, but then again, they all understood that taking in Ryuuen came with great risks. It was just that, well...I never imagined

Akito would make a move with the intention of getting the reward. I suspected he was simply trying to come up with a reason to take Ryuuen in, since no one else was willing to do so.

"What are you proposing, exactly? You're not planning to use the solidarity rule to take someone else down with you if it comes to that, are you?"

"Unless someone tries to blatantly sabotage me, I won't do that. And the rules say I can't, anyway."

The members of the hypothetical groups fell silent after hearing Akito's well-reasoned argument. And so, despite encountering a few bumps in the road, the first-years finally managed to form six groups.

This included my group, which was composed as follows:

From Class C, we had Kouenji, Keisei, and me. Three people.

From Class B, we had Sumida, Moriyama, and Tokitou. Three people.

From Class A, we had Yahiko and Hashimoto. Two people.

Then, from Class D, we had Ishizaki and Albert. Two people.

Ten people in total.

Our group was clearly unlike the other five. We had a far

more even mix of students from different classes, though I supposed the group Akito was representing wasn't too far off. However, my group still needed a representative. None of us seemed to have great leadership skills, and no one was stepping forward to claim the role. With no one around to take the lead and guide everyone toward a consensus, we all sat there, not knowing what to say.

Anyway, we had to at least report to the school that we'd successfully formed our group. We could select the representative later. So the ten of us—group number six—headed over to report to the school officials.

"Even though we managed to avoid having Ryuuen, I'm still worried about getting a decent average score," said Keisei anxiously.

I wasn't certain how good the other students were either. Personally, I'd wanted to avoid being in the same group as Ishizaki and Albert, but there was nothing to be done about it at this point. Ishizaki was blatantly refusing to meet my eyes, but that didn't necessarily mean that a third party was going to notice anything was up. Most people would assume he simply thought nothing of me.

"Kouenji is going to be a problem too," I said.

If Kouenji would take things seriously, he'd be unstoppable. His athletic and academic abilities were impressive. But "take things seriously" was where things fell apart.

"I mean, he's Kouenji, but he wouldn't really do something that gets us penalized, right? If he does, maybe it's all over."

I had a feeling Kouenji would score above average, but would do it in an aimless, noncommittal way. The only certain thing about him was that his motives were impenetrable. If he remained unmotivated, our future was uncertain.

When we finished giving our report, I noticed a group hanging around. It was the one with mostly Class A students, who should've been long gone. At first, I thought they wanted to find out how the remaining five groups had organized themselves, but it seemed that wasn't the case. There were second- and third-year students waiting around, too. More importantly, so was Student Council President Nagumo Miyabi, who ruled the second-years with an iron hand.

After confirming that all the first-year students had formed their groups, he called out to me. "You guys were surprisingly quick. I thought that would take you longer."

It seemed the second- and third-year students were almost all done composing their small groups too.

"I have a proposal for you first-years," Nagumo said. "How about we form a large group right now?"

"Aren't we going to decide that tonight, Nagumo-senpai?"

"That's just the school being flexible. They didn't expect

that the small groups would form so quickly. Since all grade levels have finished, wouldn't it be best if we moved on to the next step?"

Apparently, his suggestion was unexpected—even to the teachers. Sensing that we were about to start forming large groups, the teachers began to move in a hurry. Since the student council president himself had proposed this, the other students could hardly refuse.

"You don't mind, do you, Horikita-senpai?"

"I don't. This is more convenient for us too."

Discussions were underway, with Nagumo at the center.

"So, how do we do this? Should we have a draft-pick system? One person from each of the first-year small groups plays rock-paper-scissors against the others. The outcomes determine the order in which people make their picks. Based on that order, they can choose which second- or third-year small groups they want, and thus we'll get large groups. A fair and quick process."

"The first-years don't have much information to go on. That doesn't seem fair."

"It's never going to be completely fair. We all have different amounts of information, in the end."

A brief but important conversation between Nagumo and Horikita's brother followed. There was no way a first-year could interrupt.

"What do you first-years think? If you have any complaints, speak up," said Nagumo, knowing full well that no one would talk back to him.

"We have no objections," answered Matoba, apparently now representing the first-years.

"I see. In that case, how 'bout we get started?"

Nagumo smiled, and then joined up with his own small group. The second- and third-year students reformed their groups so that it was easier for us to tell them apart. Then the representatives of five small first-year groups stepped forward. Nagumo regarded us fondly, like we were adorable children.

"Now all that's left is *that* group."

My small group was the only one that had yet to pick a representative, so naturally, none of us were stepping up to play rock-paper-scissors. I lightly pushed Keisei, making sure I wasn't noticed. He looked puzzled but then reluctantly raised his hand.

The six representatives formed a circle and started playing. Keisei was selected to pick fourth. First up was Matoba's group, which was mostly filled with Class A students. Second was Hirata's group, consisting mostly of Class C students. Third was the Class D group, represented by Kaneda.

"You can discuss among yourselves which group you'd like to pick."

Two groups that immediately stood out as top choices: the group containing the leader of second-year Class A, the student council president Nagumo, and the group led by Horikita's brother, a third-year student. But someone like Hirata, who had many friends and acquaintances across different grade levels, might be able to spot an excellent group that didn't appear to be one at first glance.

Matoba's group, the first to pick, chose the third-year group containing Horikita Manabu without hesitation. Next, Hirata carefully assessed each of the eleven groups. In the end, he didn't go with one of the two obvious choices I mentioned but picked a group of third-years that didn't have a single person I recognized.

"Hey, Hirata, you sure that's a good idea? Shouldn't you pick the student council president's or something?" Ike interrupted, unsurprisingly.

"Yes, I'm sure. I think this is a good choice. Exceptional people have their appeal, sure, but they can bring trouble in their wake. Besides, the seniors I chose aren't half bad," replied Hirata, nodding with apparent confidence.

Ike decided not to push the matter, a sign of the trust Hirata had cultivated with our class.

The majority-Class-D group was next. Kaneda consulted his classmates—which is to say he simply informed them which group he wanted to choose. There were no objections, and he made his selection immediately.

"I would like to join second-year Gouda-senpai's group, please."

Once again, Nagumo's group had been passed over.

"I wonder why they're avoiding Nagumo," I muttered doubtfully. Akito, standing next to me, offered an answer.

"Because aside from Nagumo-senpai, the other members are kind of iffy."

"Is that so?"

"Well, I suppose they're not *all* iffy, but there are a lot of C and D guys. The second-year group with lots of Class A students is the one Kaneda picked."

In other words, it wasn't that Kaneda had avoided picking Nagumo—just that he had chosen reliable, strong allies. I *was* curious as to why Nagumo hadn't formed a group of mostly Class A students. I knew he controlled all the second-years; bringing members of his own class together seemed like a more reliable option.

Finally, it was Keisei's turn. "Is it okay for me to decide?" he asked the rest of the group.

"I don't care. Don't really get it, anyway," said Ishizaki.

It seemed Ishizaki, and by extension the Class D students, were fine with leaving the decision to Keisei. The Class A students had no real opinion on the matter either. The Class B students said nothing at first, but after thinking it over for a while, they made the following request.

"Please pick Nagumo-senpai's group."

Though Nagumo's group was mostly composed of Class C and D students, I was guessing it was the presence of the council president that made them rate it so highly. After hearing the Class B students' request, Keisei chose Nagumo's group.

After that, discussion came to an end. The six large groups had formed successfully.

"Horikita-senpai, since we're in separate large groups, how about we have ourselves a little contest?" proposed Nagumo. Horikita shot him a sharp look.

I heard a somewhat exasperated sigh, and a third-year named Fujimaki stepped forward to admonish Nagumo. I recognized him as the person who'd taken charge during the Sports Festival, meaning he wielded a certain degree of influence.

"Nagumo. How many times have you done this? Enough already."

"Whatever do you mean, Fujimaki-senpai?"

"You keep challenging Horikita to competitions. I've never interfered before, but this is a large-scale special exam that includes the first-year students. You cannot treat this like your own personal game."

"Why do you say that? Distinctions like first and third year no longer apply right now. Challenging someone under such conditions is hardly unusual, is it? There's nothing in the special exam rulebook to forbid it." Rather than cower before Fujimaki's impressive bulk, Nagumo chose to taunt him.

"We're talking fundamental morals here. Even if something isn't expressly against the rules, some actions are good, and some are bad. That's obvious."

"I don't really think so. If anything, it's precisely seniors like you who hinder the growth of younger students by refusing to do battle with them, wouldn't you say?"

"You may be student council president, but that doesn't mean you can do as you please. You need to be aware of the fact that you're overstepping your authority."

"If you think that's the case, then please, *make* me aware of it. How about *you* be my opponent, Fujimaki-senpai? You're third-year Class A's number two, aren't you?" replied Nagumo, stuffing his hands arrogantly into his pockets, acting as though Fujimaki were an afterthought.

It was cheap provocation, but it seemed to successfully antagonize some of the third-years. A few students started to step forward. However, Horikita kept them back.

"I have rejected your demands until now," Horikita said. "Do you know why?"

"Hmm, let's see. I'd say it's because your friends are scared you might lose, but that can't be right. You are superior to every other person I've met, Horikita-senpai. You're not afraid to lose. You never even *think* that you could lose."

The second-year students listening to Nagumo wore worshipful looks on their faces. He wasn't a friend or a patron. He was a rival, a hated enemy, but also someone they deeply respected. It seemed he inspired a variety of powerful emotions, anyway.

In the two years he'd been at this school, Nagumo had accomplished many things that no ordinary person could. Not even the third-year students could comprehend the extent of his achievements. The first-year students even less so.

"I'm the same as you, Fujimaki-senpai. I don't want any futile conflict either."

"The conflict you *do* want gets too many other people involved."

"But that's just how this school works. And I think that's the best part of it... Well, I suppose it comes down to a difference of opinion. At any rate, I wish we could have had a little showdown in that relay during the Sports Festival, senpai. Alas, that didn't happen. I'm still really frustrated about that, y'know?"

"I can't imagine what a showdown between the second- and third-years would do to help us in this exam."

"You're probably right. You're that kind of person, senpai. But all I want is a battle between the former student council president and the current student council president. You're going to graduate soon. Before that happens, I want to see whether I've surpassed you."

There was no telling if Nagumo would ever stop. It was like he was possessed by some kind of unceasing longing.

"What would the battle even be?" Horikita asked.

The third-year students looked shocked at the implication he might be about to accept Nagumo's challenge.

"How about which of us can get the most students expelled?" replied Nagumo.

Everyone, from first-years to third-years, started murmuring amongst themselves.

"Stop joking."

"I really do think that would be interesting. But if you insist...how about which group can earn the higher average score? Simple and easy to understand."

"Very well. I accept."

"Thank you. I knew you wouldn't disappoint, senpai."

"However, this is a personal battle between you and me. Don't drag anyone else into it."

"Don't drag others into it? Given the rules of this special exam, I would think getting someone to drag your opponent's group down was a valid strategy."

"That's the very opposite of what the essence of this exam is meant to be. This is, at most, an exercise to test our group's unity. The point of the test isn't to exploit a weakness in an opponent's group, even if you happen upon one by accident."

"...What does that mean?" said Ishizaki, seemingly directing his question at Keisei.

"It means we play fair and square, based on our abilities and nothing more. To put it simply—no dirty tricks. No kicking our opponents while they're down, like Ryuuen likes to do," Keisei answered.

"I see."

Ignoring Keisei and Ishizaki, Horikita's brother and Nagumo continued with their discussion.

"If you don't agree to my conditions, I won't accept your challenge," said Horikita. In all likelihood, the ultimatum was meant as a way to hamstring Nagumo.

"So I can't win by attacking Horikita-senpai's pawns, huh? Fine." I'd expected him to object, but surprisingly, Nagumo agreed readily enough.

However, Horikita's brother wasn't finished.

"This isn't limited to my group. I refuse to acknowledge any methods that cause harm to spill over to other students either. Our competition is invalid the moment I determine you've been meddling in others' affairs."

"Just as I'd expect, senpai. You miss nothing. I'd considered recruiting other groups to launch a joint attack, but..." Nagumo smiled audaciously. "Well, since I'm the only one who really wants to compete, I don't mind agreeing to a certain number of conditions. All right. Fair and square, let's see who scores higher and works better as a group or whatever. Ah, let me say this, though—no need to penalize the loser, yeah? After all, our pride is what's on the line here."

Horikita's brother said nothing to either confirm or deny that. That probably meant he didn't even intend to put his pride on the line for this.

2.4

• •

WITH THAT, the long opening act was finally at an end. But then Nagumo called out to our small group, stopping us in our tracks.

"Hey. Now that the seniors are gone, it looks like you guys haven't decided on a representative yet."

"Huh? How could you tell?" asked Keisei, sounding slightly panicked.

"When I suggested everyone play rock-paper-scissors, it took a minute before you stumbled out. If you'd had a representative picked, he'd have stepped forward right away. I noticed one other group had a delayed reaction too. I'm thinking the groups that couldn't decide on their representatives were probably the ones with a more balanced mix of three or four classes," said Nagumo.

Nagumo probably didn't know each and every one of

the first-year students. Even so, he had correctly deduced how our groups were divided, which wasn't something just anyone could do. Any delays on our part had been minor. We hadn't discussed it; I'd just shoved Keisei and he'd immediately stepped up. Most people would never have noticed anything wrong.

I'd been trying to avoid exposing what could be construed as a weakness in our group. I guess my attempt had been in vain.

"I thought the school didn't mind if we decide on a representative later."

"That's right. But we want to know who the first-year representatives are. I want everyone to be aware that it's better to select a representative early on. The later someone assumes that role, the more time they have to spend playing catch-up."

I wasn't sure how accurate that was, but Nagumo's meaning was clear. He wanted us to select our representative now.

"...What do we do?" asked Keisei, directing his question to the group. Other than me, he wasn't very familiar with its members and probably didn't want to be pushed into the role.

"However you decide is fine. Pick a representative now."

If the student council president was giving us a direct order, then even ostensible delinquents like Ishizaki and Albert couldn't object.

"No one's gonna volunteer for this. How about we go with rock-paper-scissors again?" said Ishizaki, balling up his fist. I agreed.

The nine of us formed a circle. Nine fists. That meant we were short one person.

"Hey, Kouenji," said Keisei. Kouenji was looking out a window and didn't even bother acknowledging us.

"Blondie. Hurry it up," said someone from the second-years, their voice containing a hint of anger. Kouenji finally turned around—and said nothing about rock-paper-scissors. Only his hair.

"Heh. You find my hair to be a truly exquisite shade, do you not?"

"What?"

"Kouenji, get serious."

"About what? Is a game of rock-paper-scissors what you'd call serious?"

"Hey, first-year. Kouenji, right? Are you mocking us seniors?"

As expected, Kouenji was already drawing attention to himself.

"Mocking you? I am not mocking anyone. I have

absolutely no interest in you at all." He might have intended to convey that he wasn't mocking them, but of course, this had the exact opposite effect. "I will not participate in rock-paper-scissors. I have no interest in being representative."

"I'm not interested in being representative either. Neither is anyone else. But this is the only option," said Keisei exasperatedly. But Kouenji showed no sign of complying.

"You say bizarre things, boy. If you don't want to do something, then there's no reason to participate. Don't you agree?"

"No. Those are the rules."

"The rule is that someone from the group must become the representative. In that case, someone other than me will do it."

"Stop screwing around. Being selfish ain't gonna fly here," snapped Ishizaki, who once had fought with Kouenji, together with Ryuuen.

"Heh. In that case, why not go ahead and make me the group representative?" said Kouenji, brushing his bangs aside. Ishizaki froze.

"Then you'll be the leader. You're okay with that?"

"You are free to push that job onto me. I have no intention of objecting to each and every little thing. If we have no representative, then the group will be punished, yes? If you're afraid of that, I'm fine with this option," said Kouenji.

However, what he said next left everyone dumbfounded.

"I will do whatever I want to do. If I don't want to do something, then I absolutely will not do it. This means I won't be fulfilling the duties of the representative. It doesn't matter who seeks to consult me; my resolve will not waver. I may even boycott the exam. Even if that results in our scores dropping below average. Even if that results in someone being expelled. Okay?"

"That's... If you do all that, you'll get expelled too!"

"Heh heh. Yes, I suppose so."

It was like he didn't fear expulsion at all.

"However, this talk is really just silly. Even if I do get a zero on the exam, our average score is unlikely to drop to dangerous levels as long as the rest of you put forward your best efforts," said Kouenji, combing his hair.

But there was no guarantee that was true. It was just Kouenji's self-serving interpretation that the exam wouldn't be that difficult. Or perhaps he just wasn't thinking it through, because he just didn't care. In any case, his brand of *uniqueness* had been thoroughly proven for all to see.

"Talk about a weirdo. He must have a few screws loose," muttered Ishizaki, taking a step back and nodding.

However, I'd noticed a contradiction in Kouenji's words. Ishizaki and the others probably didn't see it, because there were no falsehoods in what Kouenji was saying and doing. Which meant that if he'd intentionally created that contradiction, then...

To find out for sure, I'd have to risk waiting until exam day.

"Well whatever. He probably doesn't have the guts to get a zero or anything. Just make him be the rep."

Ishizaki wanted to force the troublesome and risky role of representative on Kouenji if he could. Looking at it from another class's perspective, this meant losing the chance to earn double points. There was also the possibility of someone getting dragged down via the solidarity rule. But if Kouenji really did boycott the exam, the consequences would be dire...

"Knock it off, Ishizaki. If you keep that up, you'll be the one getting dragged down," said Hashimoto.

"But... Damn it. All right, fine, if you can get whatever you want by being a stubborn asshole, then I definitely ain't bein' representative either."

"All right," said Hashimoto, nodding in exasperated acceptance.

Nobody thought that our group would take first place, evidenced by the fact that no one wanted the role of representative. This might prove to be more difficult than I'd imagined. If Kouenji continued to act like, well, himself, we'd lose a considerable number of points. He was the chaotic element the second- and third-year students hadn't factored into their calculations.

But then someone stepped forward and interrupted our conversation to comment on Kouenji's bizarre behavior.

"Even I've heard rumors about you, Kouenji."

Nagumo, who'd never have a reason to interact with Kouenji under normal circumstances, approached him as though he had found something of great interest. Well, this was unexpected.

"I know about you too. You're the new student council president, are you not?" asked Kouenji, brazen as always.

"Act the fool as much as you like, but do you really not care about being expelled?" asked Nagumo. "The way this school's set up is a pain, but despite that aimless attitude of yours, you've gotten this far. It must be 'cause you *do* want to graduate from here. But you're fine with having the role of representative foisted on you? *And* you say you'll boycott the exam? Bullshit. You just don't want to put in the effort to reach Class A. But you don't want to be expelled either."

"Heh heh. You say some rather amusing things. How can you be so sure of my 'bullshit'?"

I was with Nagumo on this, though. Shortly after Kouenji had enrolled here, he'd been asked whether he had any intention of trying for Class A. He said he wasn't interested. That he only wanted to graduate.

He didn't want to get expelled, but he didn't want to climb the ranks either. Much the same as what I was hoping to get out of this school. Even if he held back on the exams, he'd be fine. That's why he was so self-assured.

"It's written all over your face," said Nagumo teasingly.

Kouenji laughed cheerfully. "Bravo, bravo." He applauded. *Clap. Clap.*

Then he answered honestly, almost as if delivering a confession.

"I lied because I don't want to be the representative. Please allow me to set the record straight. I have no desire to aim for Class A, but neither do I have any intention of getting expelled. In light of both those desires, I think an aimless attitude is perfectly acceptable," said Kouenji.

Nagumo apparently wasn't ready to accept that. "You have no interest in Class A, huh? That's a lie too."

"My, oh, my. Have I already been branded as a liar?"

"If you're not lying, then I'm curious about something,

Kouenji. As of now, do you have a surefire way of graduating from Class A?" asked Nagumo abruptly.

Everyone was shocked.

"Oh? You do say some rather *interesting* things. Please, dazzle me with your logic."

"You sure? If I explain the logic, then that surefire plan of yours will become unusable. No. I'll *make* it unusable. Understand?"

"Heh. I don't mind. I want to know whether or not you have any idea what you're talking about." Rather than act frightened, Kouenji smiled.

"You plan to be promoted to Class A by using twenty million points," Nagumo said. "It's a strategy everyone's considered at least once, but of course, it's not easy to accumulate that many points. Not impossible either, though. Right after you enrolled here, you looked into what happens to third-year students' remaining points when they graduate."

"Keep going."

"Upon graduation, private points are 'cashed in,' meaning they can be used even outside of the school. Their cash value in the outside world is naturally less than the equivalent on campus, but it's still quite an extraordinary system. You intend to buy private points from third-years by paying them more money than they could earn by cashing them in. Right?"

Everyone looked understandably thrown for a loop, unable to hide their shock.

Kouenji, hearing his strategy explained to him, gave a satisfied nod.

"Precisely. I came to that conclusion shortly after enrolling here. No matter how far I plummet during my time here, if I can obtain private points through legal means, I can graduate from Class A. Ever since then, school has become boring to me."

A miraculous gambit, and one available to him precisely because he was rich. Buying private points from students who'd given up on Class A, or from those whose victory was already secured, or from students close to graduation... It wouldn't surprise me if many students opted to take such a deal in exchange for guaranteed cash.

That said...buying points for the same price they'd net if cashed in, alone, would be twenty million yen. Not the kind of funds a high school student could reasonably be expected to have access to. Would people even believe him if he said he was good for it?

"Fortunately," Kouenji continued, "before I enrolled here, I had my picture and profile posted on the company website, proving I'm next in line to be president. I have tens of millions of yen at my disposal. It was easy to convince people to trust me."

"Yeah. I'm aware some second-years are planning to sell their points to you, and I bet a fair number of third-years are, too. You've gotten people to keep mum about it, but more than a few second-years have put their absolute trust in me. Some of them consulted me, asking if they should take you at your word. Of course, I said it was all right. It's not without risk, but you seem to be a fairly rich guy."

Nagumo looked over the assembled second- and third-years.

"However, that ends today," he said. "Even if he really is rich, Kouenji isn't a man you can trust. As you just saw, he lies without batting an eye. It's best not to do business with him, even by mistake. Oh, and by the way, I intend to raise this issue with the school. Purchasing private points prior to graduation shouldn't be allowed in the first place, after all."

"That's fine by me. I've merely been making plans to move up to Class A. I hadn't decided if I was going to carry it out."

Kouenji seems to have envisioned this as but one strategy of many. What an outrageous idea. Well, truth be told, it was just the one-of-a-kind strategy that only a rich kid like Kouenji could pull off.

"I thought you were weird, but you came up with that strategy all on your own, huh? Impressive," muttered Hashimoto, sounding both impressed and exasperated.

"What's Kouenji planning to do by abandoning his own strategy then?"

Several gazes fell upon Kouenji's classmates: Keisei and me. We had no idea...though one thing came to mind. A rich kid like Kouenji didn't *need* to graduate from Class A. Even if he hit upon a way to make it to Class A, he didn't need to actually implement his idea. If his only goal was to graduate—irrespective of class— then making allies and cooperating with other students *would* be rather pointless.

It would explain why he didn't care if Nagumo blew the lid on his plans. Maybe he'd even enjoy coming up with another strategy. Nagumo's insight into Kouenji's affairs was quite remarkable.

"This was the first time I've ever seen Kouenji get busted," muttered Keisei. I had to agree.

And yet...

"However, Student Council President, this only proves I have no real reason to play rock-paper-scissors for the position of representative. Now that my plans have been revealed, I can simply say I have no intention of taking on the role."

"I see."

Whatever tricks Kouenji might still have up his sleeve, his stance hadn't changed. On the contrary, he had exposed his own lie—which was also his only vulnerability—and tossed it out himself. This left us with no way to force the role of representative on him against his will. Someone with his degree of wealth and privilege had no reason to fear expulsion; I couldn't imagine his future being tarnished at all by such an event. We *could* hypothetically resort to drastic measures to railroad him into being the representative, but no one in our group dared try something of the sort. If we lost, he might take one of us down with him.

"I guess I should do it," said Keisei, raising his hand resignedly.

Some of the students from other classes reacted to that. But with delinquents like Kouenji, Ishizaki, and Albert in the group, and because we had little chance of winning, no one challenged Keisei for the nomination.

"It's settled."

Nagumo dismissed the group, and we left the gymnasium as instructed.

• •

"THIS SEEMS...a lot older than I thought it would be."

The small groups were shown to their dorm rooms, each of which had wooden bunk beds matching the number of people in the group. Ishizaki immediately walked to the bed at the back of the room and climbed to the top bunk.

"This one's mine."

"What are you talking about? You can't just stroll up and take what you like. That's not fair," snapped Yahiko.

"You know what they say. The early bird gets the worm," said Ishizaki. He snorted and lay down, sneering at Yahiko.

"We should discuss who gets which bed."

Keisei, our representative, tried to rein in the situation. Ishizaki probably meant to defy him just as he had

Yahiko, but I was standing right next to Keisei, and his gaze met mine for an instant. He'd been trying to avoid making eye contact with me, but being in the same group made that a foregone conclusion.

"Tch..."

For a moment, Ishizaki looked terrified. He hopped down off the bed.

"Okay, so. How exactly do we decide?" he asked.

Keisei tilted his head to the side, looking puzzled by Ishizaki's sudden change of heart. Ishizaki may have interpreted Keisei's warning as being a warning from *me*, which was frankly paranoid. Honestly, I didn't think it was all that strange to claim our beds on a first-come-first-served basis, really—although naturally, coming to mutual agreement after fruitful discussion would be more ideal.

"Heh heh. Well, I suppose I'll go ahead and help myself," said Kouenji, leaping up onto the bed that Ishizaki had been occupying.

"What the hell, man?!" shouted Ishizaki.

But this was Kouenji. Common sense didn't apply to him. He ignored Ishizaki and relaxed into the bed; within moments, he was as at ease as if this were his own bedroom.

"God damn it. To hell with discussion."

After what Kouenji had done, people started to call dibs on beds. Ishizaki gave up on arguing with Kouenji and claimed the top bunk of a different bed. Everyone seemed united in their preference for a top bunk, save Albert, the only heavyset person here, who settled into the bunk beneath Ishizaki without any complaints.

The unspoken consensus seemed to be that discussion was no longer how we were doing things.

"Guess this is the only spot I can take," said Keisei, securing the bed underneath Kouenji. Unsurprisingly, no one else wanted to take it. The others might not have noticed, but it was significant that Keisei was willing to do the things no one else wanted to do.

In the end, I settled on a bottom bunk beneath Hashimoto from Class A.

"Nice to meet you. Um..." Hashimoto reached his hand down from the top bunk in greeting. He didn't seem to know my name.

"I'm Ayanokouji. Nice to meet you."

"Hashimoto."

We shook hands lightly, as if promising to get along.

We were now free for the rest of the day and, as such, abandoned all pretense of group unity to just do whatever we wanted. A natural-born leader like Hirata might have tried to get us talking, but...

As for me, my feelings were fixed. While it was unfortunate that I wasn't getting to know any students from other classes better, it was also a relief to not have to deal with annoying small talk.

"This might be a stupid question, but can Albert speak Japanese? He understands Japanese, right?" Hashimoto lay on his top bunk, directing the question to Ishizaki and Albert.

"Of course he does. Right, Albert?" answered Ishizaki, peering down at his friend. However, Albert just continued to stare straight ahead in silence. "Or maybe he doesn't."

"Aren't you guys classmates?" Hashimoto laughed.

"I don't know, all right? Ryuuen-san's normally the one giving orders," replied an irritated Ishizaki.

"Ryuuen-*san*, huh?"

Ishizaki's respectful—and contradictory—use of the honorific was interesting.

"Is it true you guys had a fight and ousted him as leader?"

"God, shut up. Of course it is. Calling him 'san' was just...old habits, that's all."

Rather than come together as a group, we were already sniping at each other. I decided to escape the escalating conflict and take a walk around the building.

2.6

F INALLY, IT WAS mealtime. The first time we'd seen the girls since getting off the bus that morning.

The cafeteria was quite spacious, so much so that it even had stairs to a second floor with a view of the first. From what I saw, this place could apparently fit about five hundred- people. And it was currently packed.

"It's not easy to meet up with someone when we don't have our phones."

Horikita and Kei were probably looking for me, but I didn't set out to search for them. If they did happen to run into me, their reactions would probably be polar opposites. Horikita would probably snap at me for avoiding her, while Kei would wait and see what happened, understanding that since I hadn't sought her out, there was no reason for us to make contact right now.

Touching base with various students on the first day was to be expected. I doubted many people had eyes on me, but it was quite possible that Sakayanagi and Nagumo were watching. Even though I could say that Hirata and Satou had only been hanging out with us over Christmas, Nagumo understood that I had a special relationship with Kei.

I wanted to avoid conspicuous contact.

I stayed solo, observing who was hanging out with who. But first, it was time to eat. The strict allotted hour was precious. I carried my tray over to my seat and sat down alone. Back at school, students would be separated by grade level to a certain extent, but here, first-, second- and third-years mixed together.

Many of the small and large groups stuck together, but there were more than few students scouting for information. More importantly, this was the only place and time we got to see the girls, making it the only time couples could spend together.

"*Siiiigh.*"

I heard a cute, exhausted sigh be released near me. It belonged to first-year Class B's leader, Ichinose Honami. A bunch of guys and girls were crowded around her. I decided to sit nearby and listen in on their conversation, confident I'd remain relatively unnoticed.

"...Pathetic to be proud of taking up so little space," I muttered.

Ichinose and the others didn't react to me at all. Well, the cafeteria was crowded. They couldn't pay close attention to every single student.

"Good work, Honami-chan. Was it tough?"

"Ah ha ha. Well, I suppose it was, yeah. I thought deciding on a group wouldn't be so bad. But when people wanna fight, they're gonna fight."

"Nothing we can do about that. The other classes are enemies."

"But according to Kanzaki-kun, the boys came to a decision pretty quickly."

"Huh? Really? It took us until past noon."

The boys hadn't had an easy time of it, but it sounded like the girls had struggled even more than we had. Maybe the instructors had anticipated that, which explained why there weren't any classes on the first day.

"Do you think someone might get expelled?"

"Well, I can't say there's no reason to worry. Even though no one's been expelled from the first-year classes, we can't let our guard down." It seemed Ichinose was acutely aware of the danger.

"What should we do if someone gets taken down by the solidarity rule?"

"It'll be okay, Mako-chan. As long as we take this seriously, it's not going to come to that."

"Are you sure?"

"If that time does come, we'll all help each other out," said Ichinose gently. Though she looked the most exhausted of them all, she remained stout-hearted as ever. "Ahh... I'm beat."

She laid her head on the table. Unfortunately, that change of position allowed her to notice me.

"Ayanokouji-kuuun!"

Oh, hey, Ichinose. Didn't notice you there. If I said that, it'd come off as unnatural. It was probably best to just answer honestly.

"Sounds like you were having fun."

"Some girls find power in gossip," said Ichinose, flopping over once again.

I didn't really understand what she meant. This listlessness was kind of surprising, coming from her.

"I suppose I probably shouldn't do that, huh?" said Ichinose, sitting back up straight. I stopped her.

"It's normal to do something like that when you're exhausted," I said.

"Sorry for making you kind of uncomfortable."

I wasn't uncomfortable at all, but I couldn't speak

those words aloud. "Sounds like you got put in a tough group," I said instead.

"I guess you could say it's been tough just getting the groups together... Like, girls are really up-front about their likes and dislikes. Or rather, there are more than a few girls who are willing to just tell another girl they don't like her to her face. I suppose guys tend to keep their personal feelings on the down-low, huh?"

"They're pretty up-front about hating Ryuuen, though."

"I feel bad for laughing at that, but I guess there's no helping it. Still, isn't Ryuuen-kun tired of it too? Being disliked by everyone has to be draining."

She wasn't wrong, but the logic probably didn't apply to Ryuuen. If anything, he seemed to be taking it pretty easy now that he was no longer shouldering the burdens of an entire class.

"Don't work yourself too hard." Concluding that it would be pointless to linger, I stood up.

"I'm okay, I'm okay. My energy's the only thing I have going for me. See you later, Ayanokouji-kun." Ichinose waved gently in farewell.

One hour per day. That was the only time we'd have to talk to the girls. Even though boys and girls couldn't directly intervene in each other's affairs, I imagined this hour was designed for sharing information. The school likely intended us to use the time to gather information, strategize, and continue to fight, making it an area where well-liked and well-trusted students with strong communication skills excelled.

"I'm not suited to this at all."

Just like on the deserted island, there was basically nothing I could do to help.

3

HUMAN NATURE PUT TO THE TEST

It was past six in the morning when lighthearted music began to reverberate throughout the room from speakers, clearly a signal for us to get out of bed. The room was still dark. I couldn't even see sunlight through the thin curtains.

"The hell? God, shut up."

Ishizaki's grumblings were the first words that we heard. Some students lay in bed even after hearing the music, but most of us slowly started to rouse, sitting up in bed, putting on our glasses, and so on.

"I guess we're getting started," Hashimoto muttered with a sigh.

"For the time being, it'd be best if we all get up. If even one of us is absent, we'll get hit with a deduction," said

Keisei, putting on his jersey. As long as we shared a room, collective responsibility was unavoidable.

"Hey, Kouenji's not here."

"Good morning, gentlemen. Were you about to search for me?" said Kouenji, entering the room covered with a thin layer of sweat, wearing a pleasant smile. Apparently, he'd gotten up even before we did.

"Doesn't seem like you went to the bathroom or anything."

"Heh. It was such a nice morning, I went ahead and did my training."

"What training? There's no telling what we're facing today. I can't approve of you pointlessly exhausting your stamina," said Keisei. Not that Kouenji was listening. On the contrary, he offered a gleeful rebuttal.

"Even after a full session of training, I have unimaginable reserves of stamina to spare. This is nothing, really. Besides, if you are so worried about stamina, shouldn't you have warned the group yesterday?"

"I didn't...think there'd be any kind of training happening."

"No, no. I'm afraid that's not going to cut it. I remember sharing a room with you back on the cruise ship. Surely you recall that I am the sort of man who never skips out on training," spat Kouenji, as if it were outrageous Keisei would forget such a thing.

"Enough with the high-and-mighty act, Kouenji," said Ishizaki. He wasn't trying to defend Keisei—everyone was just fed up with Kouenji, who'd been behaving selfishly from square one. He was probably used to being a disruptive element.

We didn't have time for this now. The thing I most wanted to avoid was being late on the first day. Someone like Hirata would have gotten the group in order, but without a clear leader...

"Enough already. Promise us you'll cooperate."

"What do you mean, 'promise'? Have you sworn allegiance to this randomly selected group? I don't see it that way."

"Well I don't wanna cooperate, either," said Ishizaki, scanning the room and unintentionally settling his gaze on me.

"Because of Class A? Is that the reason why you hate this?" asked Hashimoto, coming down from the top bunk to stand next to me. Ishizaki's gaze settled on him.

"Tch. It ain't just 'cause of A. It's everyone," said Ishizaki. He turned back to Kouenji.

"You seem to be heading down the same delinquent path as Red-Hair-kun," Kouenji said. "It's been amusing to watch, but now that I've dealt with you directly, I've frankly had my fill. Shouldn't you hurry along to the meeting place? Leave before your incompetence is exposed."

The fact that the only person here who grasped what was happening was Kouenji just added fuel to the fire. He was choosing his words to agitate Ishizaki, and it was working.

"All right, bring it on! Yaaaah!" shouted Ishizaki.

Keisei checked the clock as Kouenji mentioned time and started panicking. "We don't even have five minutes until assembly. Leave the fighting for later."

"Ain't my problem. If we're late, it's his fault!"

It looked like no amount of water could douse the fires of Ishizaki's anger now. On the contrary, the flames were just growing hotter. Keisei could see what was happening, but he didn't know how to manage their feelings in a way that would let him wrap this up.

"You've got a one-track mind. That's probably why you got demoted to Class D," Yahiko commented, only adding more fuel to the fire. The Class B students just watched, waiting for the situation to blow over.

"This is pitiful. I don't know whether we'll make it with these clowns." Hashimoto sighed. "Well, guess there's no helping it."

The way he said it made me think he was washing his hands of the matter, but then he punched the wood of his bed frame with his balled fist. Everyone except Kouenji reacted to the sound.

"Just calm down, you lot. It's fine to duke it out, but this is the worst possible time and place. Get it? If our furniture gets banged up, we'll be held responsible. And if someone's face gets bruised, we'll be in trouble for it. Right?"

Having cut through the silence with a sound other than his voice, Hashimoto said what needed to be said. Ishizaki, who had been hollering about how our problems didn't concern him, had to understand now that he was putting even himself in jeopardy.

"Hey, Four Eyes-kun. What's your name again?"

"Yukimura."

"That's right. It's just like Yukimura-kun said. There's no time. So how about you bury that anger deep, deep down, and we go to assembly? If you're still mad after breakfast, you can decide if you want to beat each other up. That's what being a group is about, right?"

"You should be happy, Kouenji. You get to live a little longer."

"Oh, my, yes. I happen to be a pacifist," said Kouenji.

Just what you'd expect from Class A, huh? I didn't know exactly where Hashimoto fit in the class hierarchy, but he'd expertly solved this problem for us. The fire was still burning, but it was contained for now. We left the room, still cradling a bomb with a lit fuse.

The boys from all three grade levels gathered in one classroom. Approximately forty people, give or take. You could almost say it was like we made one class. The first-year students all extended brief morning greetings to the second- and third-years. Not too long afterward, the teacher entered the room.

"I'm Onodera, the instructor in charge of third-year Class B. We're going to take roll call now, and then you will go outside and clean your designated areas. After that, you will clean the school building. These cleaning duties will be part of your morning routine for the next week. In the event that it rains, you will be exempt from working outside but not let off work; you'll just spend twice as much time cleaning indoors instead. As for your lessons—they won't just be taught by school instructors. There will be individuals coming in to cover a variety of different topics. Please give them a proper welcome and behave yourselves."

With that brief explanation, our group went off to clean.

3.1

• •

THE SCENT OF SOFT RUSH from the tatami mats tickled my nostrils. The space before me made me feel strangely nostalgic. The teacher had escorted us to a spacious dojo, where it seemed we'd be working alongside some other groups.

"Starting today, you will practice *zazen* here in the mornings and evenings."

"*Zazen*? I myself have never before engaged in such an activity," said the Professor from the other side of the dojo.

The man in charge, hearing this comment, approached the Professor.

"Wh-whatever do you want with one such as I?" asked the Professor, looking up at the man. He looked unnerved by the silent, almost intimidating aura the man radiated.

"The way you speak. Is that something you were born with? Or is it a hometown dialect?" asked the man.

"Mayhap I would say that is not the case..."

"You're not a time traveler from the Muromachi Period or the Edo Period, are you?" asked the man.

"Huh? No, of course, I myself have never engaged in the luxury of time travel..."

"I see. I don't quite understand what you think you're achieving by talking like that, but here's some advice. Fix that ridiculous speech pattern and grow up."

"Wh-what?"

"What would someone think of you if you spoke that way to them upon your first meeting? Do you need me to elaborate?"

I didn't know why the Professor chose to speak that way, but even I could tell it was a deliberate affectation. He certainly wouldn't be permitted to speak that way in the real world, or at the very least, in a formal setting. There were no rules against it, of course, but it went against socially accepted codes of morals and manners. You could dig in your heels and defend it as a personal quirk, but very, very few people could successfully get away with that.

"All right, listen up, and listen well. There are people out there who sling their words and actions around without consideration for others in an attempt to stand out. To show that they're special. This is true not only for the young, but also for the elderly too," our instructor said sternly. "You don't need to change your personality to be a part of society. You're free to express your individuality, of course, but you must take other people's feelings into consideration as you venture out into the world. These lessons will help you cultivate that mentality, using techniques such as *zazen*. By bringing your words and movements to a halt, you will be unified with the people around you, merging with the group. Consider others, and finally, think. What kind of person am I? What can I do?"

He deliberately directed his gaze over toward the Professor, as if to say, 'Get it now?'

"I-I have felt fe—ack, gotta be careful."

He might not be able to get rid of his speech pattern right away, but practicing *zazen* might teach the Professor to look inward—for instance, at why he'd slipped just then.

The groups were seated individually and then given a brief explanation. This room was called the *zazen* dojo. While in here, we were to ball either our right or left hand into a fist and wrap the other hand around it. We had to keep it that way whether walking or standing. Also, we needed to keep it at the height of our solar plexus. That was a stance known as *shashu*. Depending on which sect you were in, there were different rules about how to form your hands.

We received an explanation on one more thing regarding *zazen*. Simply, it was nothing more than one form of meditation. Practicing *zazen* wasn't about emptying your head but about forming an image. There was also something known as Ten Bulls, a series of poems and accompanying pictures that illustrated the path toward enlightenment.

I was new to this *zazen* stuff, myself.

"After you've crossed your legs, place your feet on your thighs. Practice a lot, because sitting in the lotus position will have an effect on your exam results."

"Ow. Wait, for real? I can't even get one leg up."

"If you are unable to do it at the start, you may instead use half-lotus position, with just one leg crossed."

The man in charge demonstrated the pose. I was able to cross my legs without any problem, so I decided to go with the lotus position. Surprisingly, it seemed a lot of students couldn't do it...though Kouenji, who was starting to intrigue me, had his legs crossed effortlessly. He wore a faint smile, looking as though he'd already entered a state of zen.

Since his posture needed no correction, the man in charge moved past him without complaint.

"He can really do it, huh," said Tokitou in a hushed voice. He was also able to pull off the lotus position.

"He doesn't appear to dislike this kind of thing. That's a relief."

"Yeah."

Our instructor was a scary-looking guy, but this was Kouenji, after all. He might have simply refused to do the lesson.

Now that all of the students had grasped the general idea, *zazen* time began. However, since we'd spent quite a bit of time having things explained to us, our first session was limited to just five minutes.

3.2

● ●

AFTER MORNING CLEANING and *zazen,* it was around seven o'clock—breakfast time. But we were led outside instead of into the large cafeteria we'd used yesterday evening. There, we found a spacious eating area prepared for us. Several groups had already arrived.

"The school will provide a meal for you today, but starting tomorrow, provided that the weather is clear, you will be making breakfast with your group. You must discuss how you wish to divide the work with your whole group."

"For real? I ain't ever cooked a meal before," grumbled Ishizaki.

But if that was the rule, then there was no avoiding it. Preparations for breakfast were underway while we received instructions on how to prepare food from tomorrow onward. It looked as though the breakfast menu had already been set, and handouts on how to prepare the items were being distributed. At least we'd know what to cook.

"Ugh, is this all there is?"

The meal was simple. A Japanese breakfast, consisting of soup, rice, and three other dishes. For students with hearty appetites, this wasn't going to be enough. While it seemed we could choose to swap in other dishes, we'd need to prepare everything ourselves.

"Thank goodness for that island test. Compared to that, this is luxury," said Keisei, sounding somehow relieved, as he began eating.

"If we're going to do this fairly, let's have each grade level take turns at cooking," said a third-year boy who appeared to be a representative, addressing his mealtime rotation proposal to Nagumo.

"Yeah. I've got no objections. I'd like to start with the first-years."

"How about it, first-years? Any objections?"

There was no way anyone *could* object. Assuming we had clear weather for the remainder of our time, we'd be making breakfast six times. The order in which we'd be cooking would be different, but that wasn't reason enough to complain. I wouldn't say it was unquestionably the kind of thing underclassmen should knuckle under and accept, but I was fine with it.

"We accept," said Keisei.

"Since we'll be cooking breakfast, what time should we wake up tomorrow?"

"To make sure we have enough time, let's wake two hours early," proposed Keisei.

Ishizaki vigorously rejected the idea. Keisei's proposal meant he'd have to be up and ready to go by 4:00 a.m.

"Still, we don't have any choice. If we can't prepare breakfast, it'll be awful."

"Then you guys do it. I'll be sleeping."

Ishizaki had never made such statements while under Ryuuen. But in this group, he'd already risen to the top of the hierarchy. It was interesting how his behavior had changed when his status did. Being celebrated as one of the *distinguished* few who had overthrown Ryuuen probably had something to do with it.

I couldn't really blame him for being standoffish with me, given I knew what had really happened. Also, being placed in the same group as me must have shaken him. His actions and words weren't just hurting other people; they were hurting him too.

Ishizaki and Albert weren't cut out to be leaders or strategists. They were more suited to be third in command., the ones corralling the rest of the students. Ryuuen should have made sure they kept those roles—though, to be honest, Keisei and Yahiko were similar. They weren't as foolhardy as Ishizaki, but they weren't qualified to be leaders, either.

I would've thought Class B would take a more active role, but they'd been unusually quiet so far. Maybe they weren't as proactive as I thought, with the exception of certain individuals like Kanzaki and Shibata.

That made Hashimoto the person most qualified to hold the group together. His prestigious Class A position, together with his ability to assess situations clearly and communicate effectively, were all key. However, he didn't seem willing to lead.

• •

A FTER OUR PLAIN—no, our *healthy* morning meal—
the real lessons began. Our large group gathered in a
classroom that was a bit more spacious than those in the
Advanced Nurturing High School. I wondered if it was
supposed to resemble a college classroom.

There was no assigned seating, so it was inevitable that
students from the same grade level would cluster in small
groups. You could sit in the corner by yourself, but that
might gain you unwanted attention from other grade levels. You might even get a warning. Since the second- and
third-year small groups hadn't arrived yet, we first-years
had our pick of seats.

"Would it be better to sit up front?"

"No, we should probably wait before taking out seats.

Shouldn't the seniors take their seats first, and then we grab whatever's available?"

Keisei didn't want to run the risk of getting chewed out.

"Don't go being selfish again, Kouenji. You might end up sitting off by yourself."

"If we're free to choose our seats, I believe I shall sit wherever I please."

Despite saying that, Kouenji showed no sign of sitting down. So he wasn't *entirely* an agent of chaos after all. He did actually listen quietly during our normal lessons too. The man just lived by his own rules.

"Seems like you first-years are struggling a bit," said a second-year student. "Need any help?"

"We're okay," replied Keisei, lightly bowing in response. "Ugh. Why do I have to be the representative?" he muttered.

After all, communicating with the second- and third-year students was the representative's responsibility. Keisei seemed to be under a large amount of stress. If I left him hanging like this, it would only be a matter of time before he exploded.

3.4

• •

IN THE AFTERNOON, we had PE—or rather basic physical fitness conditioning. We were told the main focus would be marathon training, and that a long-distance relay race was scheduled for the last day, undoubtedly part of the final exam. We'd practice outside for a few days, and then later on the track.

"Huff huff," panted Keisei.

The many tasks we'd already completed since morning had depleted our stamina, and he was struggling. I could have helped him with a knowledge-oriented problem, but when it came to physical fitness, there was nothing I could do but watch.

Surprisingly, Ishizaki and Albert had more stamina than the average student. They made it through practice easily, perhaps because, delinquents though they were, they didn't smoke.

"All I've done since morning is analyze things."

For whatever reason, I was growing tired of this. Putting aside the question of whether I intended to play an active role, I'd come to the realization that I wanted to improve our group's performance enough to keep us safe from expulsion. If we came in last place and scored beneath the minimum threshold set by the school, then Keisei would be expelled.

The likelihood of him taking me down with him was almost infinitesimally low but not zero. If we lost, he might resent me for not offering a helping hand despite seeing him struggle. Should I provide the bare minimum of assistance necessary to save him? Or should I work to put the group on the right track? Maybe I should just observe everything and hope that the problem resolved itself? No—I quickly eliminated that last option.

Kouenji's presence would be a cause for concern too. I should probably make a move sooner rather than later.

I slowed down in order to run alongside Kouenji, who was jogging nonchalantly. Even as I approached, he didn't even glance at me. He wouldn't leave his own private world unless I forced him to.

"Hey, Kouenji. Can't you go a little easier on them all?"

"By them, you are referring to the group, Ayanokouji Boy?"

"Yeah. They're confused. Not everyone is as incredible as you."

"Ha ha ha, I certainly am one of a kind. However, wouldn't it be the absolute height of stupidity to hold myself back in order to keep pace with common riffraff?"

"Well...I don't know if that's right. But..."

"What are you trying to say?"

"It would be nice if the group could score reasonably well. I'd like to avoid expulsion."

"If that's what you want, then you must work hard to make it happen, hmm?"

"I'm saying this to you because I intend to work hard."

Kouenji didn't respond, leaving our pounding feet as the only sound we heard. He'd gone right back into his own little world. Guess talking to him was a wasted effort after all.

Half-assed threats or pleas were meaningless when it came to Kouenji. Reflecting on everything that had happened so far told me that much. It didn't matter if the class joined forces to plead with him or if the teachers put their weight behind us—if he didn't want to do something, that was that. He was an obstinate, utterly self-involved person.

3.5

● ●

PERHAPS BECAUSE it was our first day of classes, or because our marathon training had been so demanding, the rest of the lessons consisted solely of explanations for what to expect this week. It was, however, made clear to us that the primary goal of these lessons was to teach us socialization skills.

Of course, the first-years had no idea what that meant. The second-years, on the other hand, seemed to take it calmly in stride. The experience gap between us was impossible to ignore.

"Ugh."

Our final lesson for the afternoon, *zazen*, had ended. Keisei collapsed, unable to move.

"Are you okay?"

"I'd like to say I am, but my legs feel all numb. Please... give me a minute."

Looked like the lesson had been unexpectedly hard on Keisei. He remained stiff and motionless for about two minutes, waiting until the numbness in his legs subsided. Ishizaki hadn't done so well with *zazen* either. He bent forward in agony.

"Damn. Okay, food and bath. Yeah, bath. Give me a hand, Albert."

Albert approached Ishizaki, grabbed his arm, and pulled him up.

"Gah! More gently! Let go!"

Thud! Ishizaki collapsed.

"Gaaah!"

I couldn't help but be amused by watching that interaction play out. The rest of our group, however, just found Ishizaki and those like him a pain in the neck. Keisei moved to leave, ignoring them, but I purposefully held my ground.

"They're an amusing duo, huh?" I asked, deliberately drawing Keisei's attention.

"Kiyotaka, just leave them alone. They're goofing around. Don't look at them too much or you'll draw their attention." Keisei moved in front of me, blocking my view. "He might not be as bad as Sudou, but Ishizaki's still the type to punch first and ask questions later. This might end up being like Ryuuen all over again."

"Still, we're in the same group. I'm sure they won't mind a certain amount of contact, right?"

I pointed. Ishizaki noticed us and glared. Keisei flinched, but Ishizaki just left the dojo, dragging Albert with him.

"What?" I asked.

"You're surprisingly bold, Kiyotaka."

That was because I knew what was really going on with Ishizaki and his posse. I wanted to find a way to indirectly tell Keisei not to worry too much about it. As long as he was in charge of our group, he had to maintain a certain degree of control over the students from other classes.

"Keisei, we need to peel another layer off this school."

"A layer? What do you mean?"

"We might need to befriend Ishizaki and Albert to at least some degree."

"That's ridiculous. We're in the same group, but we're still enemies. I can't befriend them."

Like Keisei, I'd also believed there was no way rival classes could ever get along when I first enrolled here. In fact, the school encouraged us to compete with each other. Lately, however, I'd begun to imagine another way forward.

"It seems Student Council President Nagumo has been able to bring people together, irrespective of class," I said.

"That's...because he's charismatic," said Keisei. "Or he's just special. I don't have that kind of talent... In fact, that's not something anyone outside of Class A could even do, right? We don't know what Nagumo-senpai's planning, or if his methods will work all the way to graduation. But no matter how much he unites the second-years, the ones who graduate from Class A will have the last laugh. The rest will be left in tears." With that, Keisei left the dojo.

3.6

●●●

AFTER DINNER, I decided to head back to the room before the others. There were a few people gathered in the hallway, both guys and girls, making me think something was wrong.

"Sorry, sorry. Are you okay?"

"Yes. No need for concern."

Yamauchi, a member of my class, reached his hand out apologetically. It looked like he'd knocked over Sakayanagi Arisu from first-year Class A. She didn't take Yamauchi's hand but instead tried to get up herself.

She couldn't do it unaided, though, so she grabbed her cane, which lay on the ground. Then, leaning against the wall, she slowly got back up. It didn't take her long, but with everyone staring at her, it probably felt like an interminably long time to Sakayanagi.

Yamauchi awkwardly retracted his hand.

"So, uh. Guess I'll be going?"

"Yes. Don't mind me."

Sakayanagi smiled lightly and looked away from Yamauchi. Everyone began to disperse, looking relieved the issue hadn't escalated.

"Sakayanagi-chan sure is cute, but she's also clumsy," muttered Yamauchi. Apparently, it hadn't even occurred to him she might've fallen because *he* bumped into her.

Somehow, Sakayanagi's gaze had found mine. "Are you okay?" I asked her as I approached.

"Thank you ever so much for your concern. However, it's nothing major."

"I'll talk with Yamauchi later."

"Well, he didn't do it on purpose. I just fell, that's all," said Sakayanagi with a chuckle. But her eyes weren't laughing. "Well, then. Please excuse me."

Kamuro was usually by her side, but wasn't here. She'd probably been placed in a different group. I had no way of knowing how things were going with the girls, and I didn't care, either. However, as Sakayanagi started to leave, she stopped and glanced back at me. Did she feel me staring?

"I remembered something I wanted to discuss with you, Ayanokouji-kun."

She tapped her cane once, a thin smile on her lips.

"Class B is quite unified. Ichinose Honami-san has earned the trust of her comrades by giving it her all. However, what if they're trusting her too much?"

"That has nothing to do with me," I replied.

But Sakayanagi continued, not caring what I said.

"There was a rumor going around about her. She's said to possess a tremendous number of points, despite her lack of significant achievements—enough points to even warrant an investigation by the school, I hear. It shouldn't be possible for a single student to earn so many points alone. She's likely the treasurer for Class B. Don't you think?"

"Who knows? Only Ichinose or her classmates could answer that question. Why tell me this?"

"I'm saying, is it wise to entrust her with all of those private points? For example, if she suddenly needed a large number of points to protect herself after making some mistake, or to save a classmate, no one would blame her for it. Perhaps she's acting as treasurer for that purpose."

"Probably, yeah."

"However, if she squandered a large sum of points purely to serve her own goals, the school might investigate on the basis of fraud."

In any case, this wasn't about me. This applied to no one else but Ichinose and the students of B Class. If Ichinose really was acting as their treasurer, then the students who had deposited their points with her would be the ones who had the right to complain about it.

"I can't imagine Ichinose using private points for selfish reasons, though," I said.

"I suppose that's true. At the very least, no one doubts her. Yet." In other words, she was implying that might change. "I do so look forward to finishing this special exam and going back to school."

Looking satisfied, Sakayanagi turned and walked away without looking back.

3.7

• •

THERE WAS ABOUT one hour left until ten o'clock, which was lights-out time. None of us really had anything to talk about, so we sat around in our shared room in silence.

Breaking the ice was proving to be surprisingly difficult. Even if you made an effort to initiate conversation with someone from another class, it could easily feel forced. Ideally, someone would bring up a topic we could all chime in on, but seemed like it might be too much to hope for.

Trying to force conversation would be off-putting. If only someone would strike up a conversation.

A knock came at the door. Apparently we had a visitor.

"Who could that be?"

Everyone looked perplexed.

"Maybe it's a teacher," said Ishizaki disinterestedly.

That was certainly a possibility. Keisei got up, went to the door, and asked who it was. The answer was surprising.

"Are you still awake?"

"Student Council President Nagumo! Is something wrong?" asked Keisei.

"I came to check on you since we're in the same group. Can I come in?" asked Nagumo.

There probably wasn't a single first-year student brave enough to refuse him. Keisei immediately complied. Apparently, Nagumo hadn't come alone. Vice President Kiriyama and two other third-year students accompanied him: Class B students named Tsunoda and Ishikura.

Once inside, Nagumo scanned the room.

"It appears all the rooms are identical, senpai," he said to Ishikura with a grin.

"It looks like it. Now, how exactly do you plan to deepen our bonds of fellowship by bringing us to the first-years' room?" asked Ishikura.

The question was directed at Nagumo, but Keisei, not understanding what he meant, spoke up. "Bonds of fellowship?" he asked.

"I already told you, didn't I? I came to check on you, since we're in the same group. We don't have TV or computers or smartphones. There's nothing remotely resembling entertainment. But it's not like we have no-thing to play with," said Nagumo, pulling a small box from his jersey pocket.

"Cards?"

"You're probably thinking, 'Cards, in this day and age?' Well, cards are a staple game at camps like this."

Nagumo sat down in a random spot, peeled the plastic tape from the sealed box, and opened it.

"Take a seat, senpai. Sorry first-years, but there isn't much space. You stay in your beds," said Nagumo as some of the first-years began to get up.

"I'm not playing," said Tsunoda. He turned his back to Nagumo.

"Come on, don't say that. Let's play. It might help us chat a bit more freely," said Nagumo.

Tsunoda stopped in his tracks, seemingly giving up, and took a seat. Ishikura sat beside him.

"We should bet something to make the game more exciting. Any ideas?"

The first-year students, nervous in the presence of upperclassmen, said nothing. They didn't know how to address the student council president, and Nagumo, of course, had anticipated they would shrink back that way.

"We decided on the order in which people will making

breakfast, right?" he said. "Let's bet on that. If, for example, you lose constantly, you'll be on meal duty until the end of camp. On the other hand, if you never lose, then you never have to cook breakfast."

"Hey, Nagumo. Shouldn't we discuss that with the entire group?" said Ishikura.

"It's only breakfast duty. Come on, give me that much. Please."

He was the acting student council president for our school, and yet he was so completely casual in how he talked, even to seniors. The other third-years seemed unable to respond. They probably knew of the tension between Nagumo and Horikita Manabu and didn't want to get involved.

"Fine. Let's decide by playing cards."

"We're okay with this?" Keisei asked the other first-year, sounding slightly apprehensive. Ishizaki, Hashimoto, and the others nodded, as did I. The others eventually nodded too—except Kouenji.

"Kouenji, you object to this?"

Nagumo should've just ignored him. Their little exchange in the gymnasium this afternoon probably made him want to poke the bear.

"I neither approve nor object. The majority has already spoken."

"I don't care about the majority. I want to know what you think."

"Then allow me to answer, student council president. I haven't the slightest interest in this exchange. I don't care enough to either approve or object. Does that satisfy you?"

Kouenji's comments seemed designed to cause more problems. However, Nagumo let loose an unexpectedly amiable laugh.

"Why don't you join the student council, Kouenji? I'd love to have someone as interesting as you aboard. I've heard you're fairly accomplished in both academics and athletics too."

Everyone in the room, including the third-years, was shocked. Kouenji was the only one who didn't react.

"Well, that's quite unfortunate. I have no interest in the student council."

"I suppose you wouldn't. Well, you're welcome any time. If you do happen to develop an interest, call me. Now then, how about we get this card game started?" Nagumo looked away from Kouenji.

"What game exactly are we playing?"

"How about something simple. Old Maid? The person holding the joker in the end loses. Two players from each grade will participate in six games total."

I wasn't very familiar with cards, but even I knew about Old Maid.

"The participating students are free to switch out. Just don't switch in the middle of a round," said Nagumo, shuffling the deck.

Once he was done, he handed the cards to the third-years so they could shuffle as well. To truly ensure that no one could tamper with the cards at all, the deck was then handed over to the first-years to shuffle. Keisei shuffled while he looked at us, seeking one other student to participate. Since there were no volunteers, Hashimoto raised his hand with a look of resignation.

● ●

OUR GAME OF Old Maid with first-, second-, and third-years had begun. Each grade level was scheduled to take two turns at rising early to make breakfast. So if you played six games of Old Maid with five wins and one loss, you'd still be fine. Four wins and two losses would be okay too.

"Playing silently isn't fun at all. Let's chat," proposed Nagumo.

He received the deck back from Keisei and dealt the cards.

"I'll deal the first round. From the second round onward, the loser has to shuffle and deal."

The players nodded in agreement. Nagumo hadn't looked at me once since entering the room. Even though we'd already met during winter vacation, I apparently didn't exist to him.

"Oh, first-years who aren't playing...just relax. Pretend we're not here. Being nervous around your seniors all the time will affect your performance this week."

Nagumo could say that, but we couldn't be as relaxed as we had been a little while ago. Except Kouenji, who ignored them completely and went to sleep.

I decided to quietly observe the game to the end.

"Even though it's just a game, we can't lose to the first-years, senpai."

"Unfortunately, I don't have the best luck. If you expect too much of me, you'll be disappointed."

"It'll be fine. I think my senpai are all pretty strong. You won't lose the first or second game."

Despite this being a game where chance dictated much of the outcome, Nagumo brimmed with confidence. They were already approaching the game's halfway point.

"Done."

Ishikura successfully got rid of all of his cards. Vice President Kiriyama was next, and Nagumo was third. The second-years clinched victory quickly, adding pressure to the first-years.

"Done."

Hashimoto put down two cards with matching numbers, bowing to the third-years as he did so. The remaining players were Keisei and Tsunoda, a third-year.

For such a tense game, the players seemed rather calm. Keisei had two cards left and Tsunoda one. That meant Keisei was holding the joker. If the third-year picked the joker, Keisei would be the winner. But after some deliberation, Tsunoda picked the winning card.

"That settles it."

"I lost."

The first round ended with Keisei's defeat. The first-years had to make breakfast at least once.

"Let's keep calm. Losing once or twice isn't a big deal," said Hashimoto. Keisei nodded but seemed apologetic. He was probably worried he'd lose another round.

"Hey, I already told you, didn't I? The loser collects the cards and deals them," Nagumo said.

"S-sorry," said Keisei, collecting the cards in a panic.

The second round soon began. From where I was seated, I could see one of the third-years' cards. He had the joker. He held it until about halfway through the round but eventually passed to another student.

The final two players were Kiriyama and Keisei. Keisei couldn't help but look incredibly nervous at being in the one-on-one showdown for the second time in a row. On top of that, judging from the number of cards remaining, I knew that Keisei was holding the joker.

Kiriyama slowly, hesitantly picked a card. Keisei

struggled to keep his poker face, but he hung his head in defeat. Within the span of a few minutes, the first-year students had suffered two consecutive defeats. Yahiko, who had been watching the situation unfold, signaled to Keisei that it was time to switch.

"Probably for the best," said Nagumo. Hearing that, Keisei obediently tagged out and let Yahiko in.

"I'm not good at games like this. Sorry, we're counting on you," Keisei said, settling down to watch the first-years battle.

Of course, Yahiko was probably nervous to face off against seniors. However, perhaps because he was used to treating Katsuragi with the deference due an older student, he seemed relatively calm. Still, composure might not have helped much with Old Maid. I didn't know how much skill was involved, but you probably needed at least some luck not to draw the joker.

"I think it's time to let the first-years have one," said Nagumo, perhaps feeling slightly bad that we'd lost multiple times in a row. "By the way, Ishikura-senpai. How's the club been lately?"

"I thought you weren't interested in basketball."

"No, I am. I mean, I'm not as interested as I am in soccer."

"We had some pretty athletic first-years join, so we might expect some good things next year. We didn't really achieve much this year, pathetic as it is to admit that, as the captain."

Several first-years had joined, but he was probably referring to Sudou, whose skill had even caught the attention of even a retired third-year.

"I'm looking forward to it."

"You seem like you're devoting all your time to the student council. Don't you have any lingering attachment to soccer?"

"I wasn't planning to go pro or anything. Besides, I can continue playing soccer wherever. Being student council president here was really appealing."

"It's good that you're putting in effort as president, but I don't like you picking fights with Horikita."

"I don't mean to pick a fight. I simply want my senpai to acknowledge me, especially when I've admired him for a long time."

Ishikura shot Nagumo a glance but then looked away.

"I'm first this time," said Ishikura, laying his cards down flat.

"I'm in, too," said Yahiko right afterward. He happily placed his final two cards down. For the first-years to win, Hashimoto had to pull through. The number of cards in his hand was decreasing, but all that mattered was who held the joker.

"All right."

After another second-year student took third place, Hashimoto also got rid of his cards.

"Oh, ho, looks like the firs-years survived this time. Congrats."

"Thank you very much, Nagumo-senpai."

The final players were Nagumo and Tsunoda. However, Nagumo had the advantage, with a 50 percent chance of victory.

"Here goes," said Nagumo, claiming the card on the right. However, he'd grabbed the joker. "Too bad."

Nagumo held out the two cards in his hand. Tsunoda picked the card on the right, just as Nagumo had done.

"That settles it."

In the end, Nagumo had the joker, and the second-years suffered a defeat.

"Looks like I got beat. All right, should we start the fourth round?" Nagumo began dealing the cards, not looking frustrated in the least. "You first-years finally won a round, so how about you lose again this time? I mean, we *are* your seniors. I'd like you to take over our duties."

"If I remember right, Sudou is from Class D. Who here are Class D students?" asked Ishikura, looking around.

"Ah, we're Sudou's classmates," said Keisei, looking at me. "Oh, and we were just promoted to Class C," he added.

I didn't expect them to care much about what was going on in the other grade levels, but when Keisei said that, Ishikura looked impressed.

"Promoted from D to C, huh? That's amazing."

"Seems like the former Class D ran out of class points right after they started at this school, though."

"Yet they still managed to get promoted. What's the gap between you and Class B like?"

As someone asked that question, though, Ishikura stopped Keisei before he could answer. "Forget it. This group comprises all classes; I shouldn't be adding fuel to a fire," he said.

It certainly wasn't the best topic—and wouldn't be a fun conversation for Ishizaki, the rest of Class D, or Class B. In the end, the first-years barely spoke, while Nagumo and the third-years kept the conversation going.

It was the fourth round. After four out of the six players finished up, Nagumo called for the round to end.

"Both the remaining players are first-years. There's no need to finish, right?" he said.

No matter who won, it was still our loss. Yahiko and Hashimoto put their remaining cards back in the deck. We managed to win against the second-years just once and lost three times.

We'd only had to cook breakfast twice, but now thanks

to this round of Old Maid, the number had risen. The more we lost, the worse our burden became.

"Maybe I should switch out," said Hashimoto. No one seemed willing to replace him, though, with the feeling of defeat hanging heavy in the air.

"It doesn't matter who steps in. Anyone is fine. You," said Nagumo.

He beckoned me over. I wanted to decline, of course, but obviously couldn't. Regardless of whether he'd called on me intentionally or randomly, I had to accept.

"Sorry, Ayanokouji. It's up to you."

"Okay."

Well, three first-years had already played. It wasn't so strange that I'd been picked too. Besides, this was just for fun. Win or lose, it was just a normal game.

As we switched places, Yahiko asked me to deal the cards. I shuffled the deck and started to deal awkwardly.

"All right, this is the fifth game. I think it's about time the third-years go down. Come on, first-year," said Nagumo, trying to light a fire under our asses.

I fanned out my cards and assessed my hand. I had several cards with the same number and the joker. Unless I handed that card off to a second- or third-year, we had no chance of winning. I wasn't very familiar with playing cards, but I was curious about one thing.

In a sense, drawing the joker at the very onset might be a good thing. As I finished assessing my hand, the game began, and people took their turns in order. It seemed no one was going to draw the joker from me. Occasionally, one of the seniors would put their fingers on the card but then immediately pulled their hand back.

However, during the fifth round, someone finally took the joker from me. The senior who took it looked at me for an instant but then immediately regained his composure and resumed the game. This time, Yahiko was the first to finish, and then I finished second. The first-years were done.

"The first-years came out on top this time, huh? Maybe the tides have turned."

The game came down to a one-on-one between the remaining third-years. Exactly what Nagumo had hoped for, probably.

Only one game left. As a first-year, I wanted to avoid losing again.

"This next game's the last one."

"I'll deal," said Ishikura. As he did, Kouenji spoke up.

"Student Council President Nagumo."

"What is it, Kouenji? Do you finally feel like participating?"

"I'm feeling a *tad* bit curious, I suppose. How do you foresee this final game will end?"

Nagumo ignored Kouenji's pompous way of speaking, focusing only on the question.

"How do I foresee?" said Nagumo.

Nagumo glanced over the participants.

"Even though this is just a game, the seniors are experienced. It's unlikely the first-years are going to win," he said.

Kouenji closed his eyes and smiled, as though satisfied.

Most probably didn't understand the intention behind Kouenji's question. Only the senior students had a grasp on the situation. I agonized over what I should do. If I relied on luck alone, I was almost guaranteed to lose. However, if I attempted to influence the results, I might end up drawing Nagumo's attention.

I checked my cards. One of the cards in my hand was the dreaded joker. I had to get rid of it if I wanted to avoid defeat.

"I'd like to leave the first-years with three losses. But I'm also okay with four," said Nagumo. I couldn't imagine that statement was random.

The final round started, turns being taken in clockwise order. Every player discarded two cards. In a minute or two, the outcome would be decided.

"**S**ORRY, FIRST-YEARS, but I finished first."

That was Tsunoda. Kiriyama was the next player to finish. That left us first-year students, Nagumo, and Ishikura. The joker was still in my hand. I'd given up on winning, so I let the game continue. Yahiko finished next. He sighed in relief, hand to his chest.

Right after that, Ishikura finished. The match became a showdown between Nagumo and me.

"You don't seem to be having fun, Ayanokouji."

"That's not true. I just have a hard time expressing myself."

"Really? You've looked kind of pale ever since we started. Have you had the joker all this time?"

Nagumo's remarks weren't strange at all. Since he didn't have the Joker and I was the only player left, he obviously knew what that meant.

"You might be right about that," I replied, trying to be evasive. Engaging him directly might be bad.

I knew what Nagumo wanted from me, after all. He wanted me to talk back to him like Kouenji had.

I silently offered him the two cards in my hand. One was the joker, the other the exact card Nagumo needed in order to win. In all likelihood, Nagumo would draw the winning card. But I didn't understand the look on his face.

Nagumo smiled as he put out his hand.

And then...

"You must be glad, Ayanokouji. Looks like you escaped."

Nagumo had drawn the joker.

"Talk about a surprise. I was sure you'd draw the winning card," said Ishikura to Nagumo.

"In the end, card games come down to luck. When you lose, you lose." Nagumo shuffled the two cards in his hand, and offered them to me. "All right, take your pick."

From an outsider's perspective, I had a fifty-fifty chance, but that wasn't really the case here. Even though he'd taken the cards from a sealed box, Nagumo had been the first to deal. That was probably when he'd marked the joker. Though almost invisible, there was a minute notch on the card.

I'd arrived at this conclusion by looking at the spread of wins. In the five games so far, Nagumo had predicted the outcomes would be ahead of time, even though, with inexperienced first-years in play, there should have been no way of knowing how a game would go. But Nagumo was evasive, only saying which team had a high probability of winning and which did not.

The senior students who'd realized the trick…no, who'd been *told* about it…had an overwhelming advantage. Disgusting. From where I was sitting, the card on the right was marked, meaning it was the joker. There was no mistaking it.

If I picked the other card, though, would what happen? The answer was simple. Nothing. I'd have just won by a fifty-fifty chance.

"I can't tell which is which no matter how hard I try, so I'm just going to pick randomly. Here goes," I said, reaching out. But Nagumo pulled his cards back.

"Give it some thought before you pick."

"I don't know that thinking it over will do anything."

"Still, try," he insisted.

"I understand. I'll give it some thought," I said, looking at the cards.

Of course, I wasn't really thinking. After about two seconds, I grabbed for a card.

"I like the one on the right. I'll take that one," I said.

As fine a reason as any. Nagumo didn't stop me that time, and I drew the winning card.

"Sorry," I said, showing that I'd won.

"You lost. Huh, Nagumo?"

"Guess so. Well, we were already scheduled to cook breakfast twice anyway, so I don't really mind." He gathered up the cards that were scattered about. "That was fun, wasn't it? I think you and I might get along just fine, Ishikura-senpai."

"I wonder," replied Ishikura, brushing aside Nagumo's seemingly good-natured words and abruptly leaving the room.

"It's fine if we start with the first-years, right? Take care of breakfast tomorrow."

"Y-yes. Thank you very much," said Keisei.

The seniors cleaned up the cards, then got up and left.

"Y'know, we didn't really interact with 'em at all," muttered Ishizaki. I understood what he meant.

Ultimately, the game had done nothing but increase the first-years' ever so slight responsibilities.

CLASSROOM OF
THE ELITE

4 A PREMONITION OF DEFEAT

WE NORMALLY HAD Saturdays off, but lessons were still being held at this outdoor school. However, the timetable was slightly different from weekdays. Our lessons were only in the morning. Once those were finished, we had free time.

The special exam had started on Thursday. It was already the third day of camp, and discord was beginning to manifest within the group. It started early, just after five o'clock in the morning.

"Aah, I'm so goddamn tired!" shouted Ishizaki at the outdoor cooking area.

"So is everyone else. Ah, please measure the ingredients correctly—don't mess up the amount of miso," said Keisei, flipping through the breakfast menu the teachers had given us.

"Shut it. Why do I even gotta help make food in the first place?!" Ishizaki groused, though he kept stirring the miso to make it dissolve.

"Look, we don't have a choice. We could get hit with a penalty if our whole group's not here."

"Whatever, dude, like hell I care. God damn it. Oh."

"What was that?"

"Nothin'."

"No, that was something. Where's the salt you were just holding?!"

"I put it all in."

Keisei turned off the fire in a panic. He tasted the soup and choked.

"You put in way too much! *Ack!* It's not even edible."

If we'd given that soup to the seniors, it would have invited a *lot* of criticism. Not to mention it was probably unhealthy too.

"You have to start over."

"Screw that. You do it. Or what about Kouenji?"

"It's not like I know!"

"You're in the same class, aren't you?!"

Hashimoto shot a backward glance at the two of them fighting over the miso soup, his hands occupied by skillfully wielding a frying pan on the camp stove.

"Dude, you're really good."

"I've always cooked my own meals," said Hashimoto without a trace of arrogance. As he continued to cook up a storm, Albert approached him silently, carrying a bowl filled with whipped eggs.

"Thank you. If you're up for it, could I ask you to cut up some vegetables too?"

Despite his bulky frame, Albert skillfully brought the kitchen knife down on the cutting board, dicing vegetables with ease. We'd be feeding a lot of people, so Hashimoto kept churning out fried eggs. Clearly, he and Albert were our team's trump cards, as far as cooking went.

Meanwhile, I'd lucked out by landing the easy job of preparing the raw vegetables and tableware. There were a *lot* of vegetables to be prepped, and although I couldn't help with the frying, I felt I could at least pitch in on the dicing and chopping. I stood beside Albert and tried to communicate with him silently, just using my eyes.

Can you handle cutting? Vegetables?

Probably, yeah.

Somehow, we seemed to understand each other—at least enough that Albert handed over a kitchen knife. Thankfully, living in the dorms had led me to develop some skill with a knife. I began to dice vegetables, keeping pace with Albert.

Where had Kouenji gotten to, anyway? It'd already been half an hour since he went to the bathroom. Classes A and B each sent one student to look for him, but since they hadn't returned, it was a safe bet they hadn't found him.

In the end, Kouenji didn't return until breakfast. When he did return, all he would say was that he'd been holed up in the bathroom due to a stomachache. Needless to say, his relationship with Ishizaki was wrecked beyond hope of repair at this point.

4.1

SOMETHING HAPPENED while I was studying moral-ity during our third period that Saturday. I heard a girl's cheerful voice outside, and peering out the third-floor classroom window, saw Ichinose race spiritedly through the yard. She'd had a difficult time getting the groups coordinated on the first day, but she seemed cheerful now.

Sakayanagi had enthusiastically declared she would crush Ichinose, but I saw no sign of that happening. Of course, I could only see what was on the surface.

As I watched, I was able to discern, to a certain ex-tent, the people who were members of Ichinose's group. Surprisingly enough, I spotted only one person from Class C among them. The Class B students were all un-familiar to me, with the exception of Ichinose. Had they gone with the same approach as the boys—picking the minimum number of people from Class B in order to have an even mix of people from all four classes?

I wasn't really sure who the Class A and D students were, but I did spot the girl who had suffered a severe injury by running into Horikita as a part of Ryuuen's ploy during the Sports Festival. Fortunately, she must have made a complete recovery, for she seemed to be running just fine.

The only student from Class C, meanwhile, was a girl named Wang Mei-Yu.

She'd come to Japan from China during elementary school and had remained here ever since. At least, that's what I'd heard. Her nickname was Miichan, though only close friends ever called her that. All I knew was that she did well in class and was especially proficient in English.

Though there were some slight differences in their scores, overall, she was as academically adept as Keisei. Strangely enough, she was just as athletic as him too— which was to say she was currently dead last by a wide margin, despite struggling desperately to keep up with the group. She staggered along, breathing heavily and looking up at the sky, seeming ready to collapse.

Ichinose noticed Miichan lagging behind and slowed down. She matched Miichan's pace to run supportively

alongside the other girl, encouraging her. Soon after, another girl came up beside them. It was Shiina Hiyori from Class D. She didn't seem especially athletic either, but she had a smile on her face as she ran alongside the other girls.

According to Ryuuen and the people around him, Shiina had taken on the role of leader of the Class D girls. If that was true, then I was looking at a girls' group with two class leaders in it. With that in mind, it wouldn't have been strange for Horikita and Sakayanagi to be together too—but they were apparently in different groups.

Feeling a surge of curiosity about how those groups had come together, I gazed out the window instead of focusing on the lesson. When our instructor spoke up, though, I could tell that things were about to become difficult.

"We will now begin self-introductions. However, you won't simply be introducing yourselves. Please keep in mind that this will be one part of your lesson. From now on, you will all be giving a speech every day. The themes will differ between grade levels, but the four fundamental criteria on which you will be judged are volume, posture, content, and communicativeness.'"

The word *speech* had indeed cropped up in the syllabus we'd been given back on the bus, making this undoubtedly one of the subjects we'd be tested on as part of this special exam. I was willing to bet every member of our large group would have to deliver a speech they'd composed themselves at some point. This part of the exam would be hell for people who lacked public speaking skills.

The instructor went on to notify the first-years that they would be giving speeches on what they'd learned in their first year of school and what they'd like to learn in the years to come. The second- and third-years had to speak about their plans for the future, like attending university or getting a job.

"For real? Talk about a shit exam," spat Ishizaki. I understood how he felt, but he was being much too loud. Even the teacher seemed to have heard him, though he didn't take Ishizaki to task over it. We could do as we pleased, but we needed to remember that our actions would ultimately affect the group.

When free time rolled around, a young man approached the first-year group. Ishizaki, who had had his legs sprawled on top of a desk, instantly corrected his posture. The new arrival was Kiriyama from second-year Class B, who served as vice president on the student council under Nagumo Miyabi. He used to be in Class A, but had been demoted after losing to Nagumo, and it seemed that, deep down, he wished for Nagumo's downfall. Horikita's brother had put us both in touch.

"I think you should adjust your attitude a bit," he said.

"S-sure. Well, I wasn't really makin' any fuss or anythin'."

"I'm not just talking about you, Ishizaki. That applies to you, too, Kouenji."

Much as he might crave Nagumo's downfall, Kiriyama still had to play the part of a dutiful vice president. He had to address anything that might affect the large group's overall scores.

"We're going to be evaluated based on the test on the final day, right? I don't think taking these lessons seriously is that important."

"The written test isn't everything there is to this special exam. Haven't you considered the possibility that our instructors will be taking your behavior in class into account? And how exactly do you plan to score well on the test if you don't take the lessons seriously?"

"Simple is best. This is *me* we're talking about, no?"

"I see. You're saying getting a high score is easy for you, eh? Well, we'll see if you can make good on those boasts when the special exam comes around. You're part of this group—shouldn't you want to avoid acting in ways that make your teammates uneasy?"

"A group that's made uneasy by my actions is a group that has no value."

"You don't get to decide that, Kouenji."

"Then who, may I ask, does?"

"No one person. The whole group does. Every student here decides."

Ishizaki couldn't help but grin after hearing that, probably because he loved seeing Kouenji get told off. However, common sense wasn't going to work against Kouenji.

"I'm worth far more than the rest of you combined. An average person cannot correctly judge the exceptional."

"You're too ignorant and infantile to even be called a high school student," Kiriyama said.

Kouenji didn't flinch, but before I knew it, nearly half of the second-years had begun to encircle us. Even Ishizaki's smile faded, his face growing stiff. Threatening words could be heard being murmured around us.

"Besides, it's not just Kouenji. There's a number of you who've been causing all sorts of problems."

He probably meant Ishizaki, but I honestly couldn't think of anyone else. We'd all been taking the lessons seriously, in our own way. Kiriyama was probably lumping us first-years together because he wanted us to focus, letting us know that we'd be earning our seniors' ire if we continued to behave impertinently. Kouenji was merely the straw that broke the camel's back.

"I think that's enough, Kiriyama."

Unable to stand by and watch the situation unfold, Ishikura, a third-year, stepped in to help.

"I know you're just trying to coach them, but the way you're doing it could come off as bullying. If that happens, you'll be the one in trouble. The first-years understand the situation well enough. Isn't that right?"

Ishikura looked to us for confirmation, and every one of us, including me, nodded. Except for Kouenji, of course.

"Excellent, Ishikura-senpai. You really got a handle on things, didn't you?" said Nagumo happily. He'd been watching the whole thing go down from the sidelines. "You really are too good to be kept in Class B. Maybe you're just really unlucky, Ishikura-senpai."

"Luck, huh? Much as I hate to admit it, I think it's just that my skills aren't up to par."

"I don't think that's true. The only reason you haven't been able to rise to Class A is because there's a genius like Horikita Manabu in your way. I know you've fought the good fight for three years. There's a 312-point difference between Classes A and B right now. Even though graduation is around the corner, I think you're closing in on them."

"Are you saying you'll lead this group to victory?"

"Exactly. If you're willing to trust me, Ishikura-senpai,

we'll win this special exam. And, as I'm sure will bring you no small amount of delight, I'll help you get to Class A. We might even be able to get Horikita-senpai removed from the school. Hmm?"

"Unfortunately, Horikita doesn't seem to be a group representative. And you aren't either, are you, Nagumo? There's nothing you can come up with that would be enough to drag him down."

"It doesn't matter if he's the representative or not. There are many ways to crush him," said Nagumo with a laugh.

"Sorry. But I can't trust you. Not with the fate of Class B."

"That's unfortunate."

Nagumo had simply laid out all his plans in front of everyone. Was he genuinely that guileless? Or was he just trying to make himself *appear* guileless? I doubted it was the former.

4.2

AT DINNER, I decided to make some minor moves.

Or so I say, though all I was really trying to do was get a better handle on the girls' situation. Ichinose and Shiina being in the same group had caught me slightly off guard, and I wanted to understand what was up with the other groups.

I wanted to better understand the girls' situation, because Ichinose and Shiina being in the same group had caught me by surprise. I wanted to understand what was up with the other groups.

Kei was eating in the same place as she had since the beginning, which made it easy to get in touch. I hadn't even asked her to do that. She truly was reliable. I, on the other hand, had been grabbing random seats that just happened to be open, wanting to avoid openly engaging with Kei, just in case.

Very few students knew about my strange relationship with Ryuuen and other members of Class D, or with Kiriyama and Kei. Besides, there were enemies on the inside of whom I needed to be cautious. I checked my timing and then sat down near Kei. Just as I was racking my brain over how I would get her to notice I was there—

"Hmm."

Kei made some kind of noise, I think as a greeting? It was very soft. Apparently, she'd noticed me, even though she was enjoying a meal with her friends. In that case, I would wait patiently until she got rid of them.

She proceeded to eat her meal slowly, letting her friends head back to the room ahead of her. I'd been considering postponing this meeting if there was a chance of being interrupted. She couldn't shake her friends, but she'd cleverly manipulated them into leaving. Finally, no one was paying attention to us, and our conversation could start. Of course, we'd immediately cut it short if someone did come.

"So? It's the third day, and you finally feel like asking for my help?"

"Yes. I have too little information on the girls."

"No surprises there. Someone with a communication impairment like yours can only make contact with so many girls."

She was giving me the cold shoulder, right off the bat. A small price to pay if it helped Kei feel she had an advantage, and keep our relationship going...but I decided to be a little mean in response.

"So, you'll make it through this special exam even if you get no help from me?"

"O-obviously. I mean, who do you think I am?"

"I see. Then there's nothing to worry about."

"Well, maybe you can analyze my situation just to make sure there's nothing to worry about. Okay?" said Kei, looking anxious.

"Tell me how the girls' groups are divided."

"Ah, before we talk about that, something's been on my mind."

"Make it quick."

If we spoke too long, people might become suspicious.

"Well, I'd say it's pretty important... What's going on with that Ryuuen guy?"

"Are you worried?"

"Well, yeah. Even the girls are talking about it. Like why he quit being the leader and all. No one knows what really happened."

"Well, I wouldn't ever call Ryuuen 'gentle as a lamb,' but he's been somewhat domesticated."

"So raking him over the coals worked?"

"Raking him over the coals?"

Kei hid her vulnerability beneath a tough façade, though her fear occasionally came into view. Her curiosity probably stemmed from anxiety over the fact that Ryuuen knew her weakness.

"Don't worry about Ryuuen. He won't do anything careless. At the very least, he won't be doing anything to you, Kei," I said, to reassure her.

Kei didn't respond. Was someone else approaching us? I'd been on my guard in case that happened...but that didn't seem to be the case. I immediately sensed what was going on.

"Sorry. It's nothing," she said. I could tell she was lying.

"It doesn't seem like nothing, Kei."

"I-I'm telling you, it's nothing."

"Is that really true, Kei?"

"...Wait a minute. You're doing this on purpose, aren't you?!" She didn't look at me, but her voice sounded threatening. Maybe I'd pushed her too far. "Ugh, God. I shouldn't have given you permission to call me by my first name."

"You're the one who started that in the first place."

"W-well, yeah."

More importantly, if she was satisfied by what I'd told her about Ryuuen, I wanted to get down to business. We were well hidden among all the hustle and bustle, but if someone happened to notice us, they might become suspicious of my relationship with Kei.

"Well, I've gathered as much information as I could, more or less. Want to hear it?"

"Yeah."

"I'm going to say this up front, though—I wasn't able to get a complete picture of all of the groups like you wanted."

"I understand. I wasn't expecting that much from you."

"Okay, that's a super rude way of putting it. Even someone like you couldn't know everything about who was put into what group, right?"

"Hmm. I wonder about that."

"What? You're saying you've memorized where everyone is?"

"I didn't say that."

"What group is Shibata-kun from Class B in?"

"He's in the group of mostly Class B students led by Kanzaki."

"What about Tsukasaki from Class A?"

"He's with mostly Class A students led by Matoba."

"Th-then what about Suzuki-kun?"

"He got assigned to a different small group than the one I'm in."

"You *have* memorized everything!"

"Just the people whose names I know. But if I see their faces, I can remember where they belong."

I was grateful that this exam had forced me to memorize the names of all of the first-year students. Once we were done here, I'd probably be able to match names to faces with nearly 100 percent accuracy. As long as I hadn't missed or misunderstood something, of course.

"*Sigh*. How is your memory this good? Don't tell me you're one of those nerdy four-eyed try-hards who spends all his time studying or something."

Unfortunately, I had no idea what Kei was saying.

"Let's get down to business. What's going on with Sakayanagi and Kamuro's group?"

"They're in the same group. It's made up of students from three classes, with nine students from Class A. Class A was the first to put their groups together," explained Kei.

So, the girls had picked a similar strategy to the Class A guys. Only they went with nine students instead of twelve.

"The fact that they've only got three classes means someone didn't join in. Or maybe Sakayanagi didn't let them in?"

"They wouldn't accept anyone from Class B. They rejected the idea right off the bat. They said they couldn't trust Ichinose or something. Well, Sakayanagi didn't say that. Kamuro did."

"Not able to trust her, huh?"

"I guess you wouldn't fully trust any student from another class, but they specifically named Ichinose. But isn't that kind of weird? I mean, even *I've* heard nothing but good things about her."

If I were asked to name a trustworthy student from another first-year class, I'd have named Ichinose, without a doubt. Of course, there were probably more than a few people who'd name Kushida, if asked the same question... At any rate, I estimated Ichinose was in the running for the most trustworthy person in our grade level.

But if Sakayanagi and Kamuro's group only had members from three classes and the minimum number of students, their point multiplier would be greatly diminished. It was a strategy where absolute victory was impossible, but so was absolute loss.

"That's not fair, right? Class A should just protect themselves. They were really forceful about how they made the groups."

"Seems that way."

A solid, reliable strategy. Sakayanagi had almost certainly devised that plan. It was surprising that someone as aggressive as her would adopt a defensive strategy like this.

"So what should I do now? Set a trap or something?"

"Cheap tricks won't work in this exam. There are some people I'd like you to monitor, though," I replied, naming some of the major players.

"Hmm. That'll be pretty tough, but I'll try."

She obediently followed orders. That was Kei's strong point.

"Anyway, what's up with this exam? Do we really have to worry about things like manners and ethics?"

"I wonder. If this were a story, I'd say it was almost like a MacGuffin."

"Huh? MacMuff—"

"That's not what I said."

"I-I know that. So what is it?" She had no idea.

"It's an element that's important because it motivates the characters but is otherwise unimportant to the story itself."

"I don't understand. Look, I know you're a smart guy, Kiyotaka, so just explain things in a way that's easy to understand."

"I'm saying manners and ethics may be necessary but aren't really important in and of themselves."

Dinnertime was almost at an end. Students started to disperse.

"But this exam... Let's just say a storm is coming."

"A storm? What do you mean? Are you saying something bad is going to happen?"

"Relax. At the very least, I say no harm will come to you." Things probably wouldn't get too bad for the first-years this time. I grabbed my tray and stood. "If I need you again, I'll call."

"Understood."

With that, I decided to return to the room.

4.3

• •

As night fell on our third day, I entered the large bathhouse. Several guys were gathered in one corner; I saw not only Yamauchi and Ike but also some Class B students like Shibata. I exchanged glances with Kanzaki, who entered the bathhouse at the same time as me.

"This is a pretty unusual combination of people," said Kanzaki, surveying the gathering with surprise.

"Yeah, sure seems that way."

"How's your group? Any trouble?"

"Dunno. But I can't say it's going all that well," I replied honestly.

Kanzaki seemed unsurprised. "Well, if you have a small group made up of an uneven number of students from four different classes, there's bound to be tension."

"I wish that were all it was."

"Moriyama and the others told me. Sounds like you guys really have your hands full with Kouenji." A natural assumption, under the circumstances.

"I'm trying my best as a classmate, but I have absolutely no control over him," I said.

"Speaking of control, have you heard about what's going on with Ryuuen?"

"No, I haven't heard anything."

It was three days since Akito had entered Ryuuen's group. Even though we saw each other in the bath, on the way to the toilet, or during mealtimes, we hardly ever spoke.

"If he were scheming or something, there'd be reports. But I haven't heard anything."

If Kanzaki—Class B's second-in-command—said no rumors were going around, then it was probably true. As someone who knew the full extent of the situation, I doubted Ryuuen would try anything, but the other students probably weren't going to let their guard down for a while. Many probably suspected he would spring some kind of trap by the end of the exam.

"If you're ever in trouble, find me. I'd like for our good relationship with Class C to continue. Ichinose feels the same way, of course."

"I sincerely appreciate that."

"Ichinose seems to have a really high opinion of Horikita. More so for her honesty than her ability, though."

"Her honesty? Huh."

I didn't know if I would call Horikita "honest" myself, but Kanzaki's definition of the word might be slightly different from my own. He probably meant she had integrity. She was a firm believer in keeping her promises. You couldn't expect anything of the sort from Sakayanagi or Ryuuen.

"Oh, Kanzaki! Hey, over here!"

Shibata waved.

"Ayanokouji! You come over too!"

Yamauchi signaled for me. Unable to decline under the current circumstances, I went.

"What's up?" said Kanzaki to Shibata.

"Just having a blast with Yamauchi and the guys here. Bein' totally honest and talking about something kinda weird."

"Kinda weird?"

"We've been talking about who has the biggest thing in our grade."

"What thing?"

"Dude, isn't it obvious what we mean? You know, down there," said Shibata with a laugh, pointing at the center of the white towel wrapped around his hips.

"I see. Sounds like you're having fun." Kanzaki released an exasperated sigh at the childish competition that Shibata was engaged in.

"I mean, yeah, it's childish. But hey, it's surprisingly fun."

Kanzaki and I didn't get what was so fun about it. We exchanged glances and decided to keep our distance. When Shibata and the other started their discussion once again, Kanzaki left. Soon after, I got up to leave too. However—

"All right, who's the current size king?" Sudou, probably having overheard the conversation, showed up. He radiated confidence as he grabbed tightly me by the shoulders, preventing my escape.

"I have no clue." I dodged the question. While the majority of us wore towels, Sudou was proudly naked.

"Oh. That's what I'd expect from Sudou," said Shibata. I could tell that he was anxious.

"Kaneda from Class D's the current king."

"Kaneda? That gangly four-eyes?"

Sudou pushed past Shibata.

"Move it," he said, before joining up with Yamauchi and the others. Kaneda, who seemed to have no intention of joining in, looked uncomfortable.

"Oh, dude, Ken, you came! You're the only one we can count on!"

"Leave it to me."

Sudou, representing Class C, confronted Kaneda, who looked perplexed at being dragged into this competition.

"You wear glasses even in the bath?"

"If I don't, my vision is so bad that I can't see well enough to walk."

"That so?"

It wasn't an aggressive competition. They simply stood next to one another. The outcome of their showdown was decided in an instant.

"Hot damn!"

Sudou confidently pumped his fist as he posed. He shouted in triumph, his voice echoing throughout the bath. Kaneda fled, the sentiment "Finally, the game is over" written on his face. I was sorry he'd gotten dragged into it.

"That settles it. I'm the king!" Sudou declared.

It was unlike anyone would challenge him, having seen the power he was packing. I hoped this pointless competition was at an end, but...

"King? Don't make me laugh, Sudou," said Yahiko, challenging Sudou with a loud laugh.

Sudou just glanced at Yahiko's naked crotch before dismissing him. "You ain't no match for me."

"No, I'm not. But *I'm* not your opponent."

"It don't matter who I'm up against. The result's the same. The king is Class D's—"

"No, Ken, we're Class C now. Class C."

"Yeah, that's right. The king is Class C's Sudou Ken-sama!"

"You're just above average. You can't win against Class A's Katsuragi-san!"

Apparently it wasn't Yahiko challenging Sudou but rather the person that Yahiko idolized—Katsuragi. The man in question was sitting on a stool nearby, reaching for some shampoo. Since he was completely bald, I wondered where exactly he was going to apply the shampoo, then decided not to ask that question.

"Knock it off, Yahiko," said Katsuragi. "I have no interest in such nonsense."

"We can't let this pass. We have to win. This is about a man's pride. No, Class A's dignity is on the line!"

"What a stupid competition..."

"But that's not really true. Is it, Katsuragi?" said Hashimoto. Yahiko just looked disgusted. "Like Yahiko says, Class A's pride is on the line. What you're packing makes you the only one here that can measure up against Sudou."

Hashimoto had personally checked out Katsuragi's "thing." He clearly had confidence that Katsuragi could win, laughing boldly at the possibility of victory.

Katsuragi, however, made no move to stand.

"Bring it, Katsuragi."

Katsuragi remained calm in the face of Sudou's provocation. However, everyone else was getting fired up. They cheered, wanting to see Katsuragi and Sudou square off.

"For crying out loud. I can't even wash my head in peace," said Katsuragi.

So that meant that he really was planning on applying shampoo on his head after all, huh.

"The contest will be over in a second, Katsuragi."

"Have it your way."

Katsuragi, having determined the best way was to accept the challenge, slowly got up. Everyone let out a sigh of admiration at the sight of his large frame.

"Th-this is...?!"

Yamauchi, who was the judge, crouched down. He scrutinized each combatant, looking from one to the other, but the differences seemed almost nonexistent. Sudou offered his opponent praise as he waited for Yamauchi to pass judgment.

"Nice, Katsuragi. That's the reason they call you Class A's trump card."

"This is ridiculous..."

"All right, and the judges say—"

Yamauchi stood up.

"It's a draw!"

Unlikely as it might seem for such a thing to happen in a competition like this, Yamauchi had determinedly they were evenly matched. Ike, Shibata, and the others gathered around, ready to object, but Yamauchi's judgment seemed sound, because they couldn't determine who was bigger either.

"Are we done?" said Katsuragi.

Clearly done with being made a spectacle, he pushed past them and went back to where he was sitting.

"I hate to admit it, but I guess the two of us share first place," Sudou said.

I didn't think anyone would object to that...but we *still* weren't done.

"I had the honor of watching your valiant battle. But my, how naïve you are," said Ishizaki from Class D.

"Huh? Don't make me laugh, Ishizaki. You ain't a match for me," said Sudou with a dismissive laugh. Ishizaki was pretty much on Yahiko's level.

"I ain't your opponent."

"What?"

"You fool! Class D possesses the ultimate trump card!"

"No way. You don't mean Ryuuen?"

"No!" shouted Ishizaki. "Albert! You're up!"

The moment Albert's name was called, there was an uproar. The thought of Albert had certainly crossed everyone's minds, but they'd avoided mentioning him. Now that unspoken rule was broken.

"Hey, that's not fair!" Even Sudou, who'd been dubbing himself a king moments ago, couldn't hide his nervousness.

"Deal with it. If we're measuring who's number one in our grade, then Albert is on our team!"

Ishizaki had a point, but no one could deny a fight that crossed into international territory put us at a disadvantage. Japan's professional baseball players, for instance, were highly skilled—but if you looked at foreign players in the major leagues, the difference in physicality was obvious. Foreigners were just made differently from us, both in terms of build and genetics.

Albert approached silently. Sudou and Katsuragi were well built, but they couldn't compare to his muscular frame. Also, for some reason, Albert was still wearing sunglasses in the bath. Maybe they had some kind of anti-fogging solution applied to the lenses, because he moved with no problem.

"Damn, he's huge..."

Albert had a bath towel wrapped around his hips, so Sudou's muttered words had to be referencing his physique. Now that I saw them side by side, the difference was clear. It was like the difference between a junior high student and a college student. It followed that the same should apply to the weapons they wielded. Though it might be precious little help to him here, all Sudou could do was pray Albert wasn't packing more firepower than him.

"Bring it on!" Sudou shouted, showing no fear. As the king, he couldn't run away.

Albert didn't say a word, but he was plenty intimidating, even so. He let Ishizaki remove his bath towel. The veil had been lifted. Everyone, not just King Sudou, watched with rapt curiosity. Was this a weapon worthy of a final boss? Or, in a stunning upset, would he be wielding something minute?

It was a clash between beasts—the most primal kind of battle.

"Go, Albert!" cheered Ishizaki as Albert's fighting prowess was made clear.

"Th-this is...?!"

Unveiled before the eyes of the current king was Albert's true form, which he'd kept hidden so far. The crowd fell silent.

"I...lost."

Two simple words from King Sudou. He collapsed to his knees, struggling with overwhelming defeat. Unlike the contest with Katsuragi, there was no need for judgment here. The difference was just that extreme.

"This means Albert's...the final boss!"

Yamauchi, Shibata, and the others folded like Sudou had, their spirits crushed. No one was capable of challenging Albert. The winds of despair began to howl. Albert slowly bent over, maneuvering his large bulk as he picked up the towel and walked off. Everyone fell to their knees in despair, recognizing their horrible defeat.

"Ha ha ha. You are all amusing yourselves like *children*, it seems."

Kouenji's voice cut through the dreary mood like a knife. He'd been observing the commotion from inside the hot tub.

"The hell, Kouenji? Aren't you frustrated, too? Look at the state Sudou is in right now!" shouted Yamauchi. Sudou was still too anguished to be able to stand back up.

"I know. But Red Hair-kun put up a good fight."

"The hell, dude? Are you tryin' to say you can square off against Albert?" said Sudou, the life gone from his eyes.

"I am a perfect being. As a man, I possess the ultimate body."

"Don't dodge the question. What are you saying, *specifically*?"

Kouenji ran his hand through his hair, without getting out of the tub.

"There is no need for a competition, precisely because I know that there is *no one* superior to me. So, there is no need to war over something so pointless."

"So you say. But it's not true, is it?" said Yamauchi, baiting him.

However, Kouenji showed no signs of nervousness.

"You truly are a fool. However, it might be fun to play along with you on occasion." He swiped his hair back from his face, looking as though he intended to accept the challenge. "Now then, shall I assume that Aaaalbert-kun is my opponent in this little competition?"

Why did he say Albert's name like that?

"No. It's Katsuragi-san!" shouted Yahiko.

"Leave me out of this, Yahiko..." said Katsuragi.

"There's no way Kouenji can win if he goes up against Albert! On behalf of the Japanese people, I'm begging you, Katsuragi-san, you must defeat him!"

Well, I supposed Yahiko and Kouenji *were* in the same group. Even though he'd been seated nearby, Kouenji probably didn't know in detail the kind of fighting power that Sudou and the others held. If Katsuragi, who was an even match for Sudou, stepped forward...then maybe he stood a decent chance of victory.

"For crying out loud... All right, just this once," said Katsuragi, exasperated. He stood to represent the

Japanese people, his package swaying left and right as he did. The guys gazed at it as if they were looking upon something divine.

"A-as I thought, he really is huge. I mean, even he can't go up against Albert, but if Kouenji—"

"Heh. I see. So you're not called a king for nothing, eh?"

"Please just end this."

"However, you are no match for *me*." But Kouenji made no attempt to get out of the bath.

"Hey, hey. You ain't *scared* or nothin', are ya, Kouenji? Or are you all talk, hidin' your thing away in the tub?" Ishizaki said, trying to needle Kouenji into making a move.

"I'm not so foolish as to direct my blade toward an unworthy opponent."

"Heh. In that case, we'll break your spirit 'til there's nothin' left. Right, Albert?!"

Albert, the great foreign threat, stood next to Katsuragi. When he did so, a strange phenomenon occurred: Katsuragi's thing looked small in comparison. Upon seeing that, Kouenji's expression changed dramatically for the first time.

"Bravo!" He clapped his hands. "I see, I see. As I would expect of the one representing the rest of the world, it would appear that you aren't all talk."

"Do you get it now, Kouenji? How much of a clown you are?"

"I've had enough of this," said Katsuragi. After he finished washing off his body, he entered the tub and kept his distance from Kouenji. Everyone ignored him, now completely absorbed in the battle between Kouenji and Albert.

"Normally, it is not my policy to show it to men. But this is a one-time deal."

Kouenji stood, grabbing a towel and wrapping it around his hips to conceal his weapon.

"S-so you really gonna do it, Kouenji?"

The ultimate eccentric and the king were going head-to-head.

"I've known the outcome of this battle from the start. Now everyone here shall bear witness too."

Kouenji struck a pose as he removed the towel that had been concealing his lower half. In that instant, a dazzling light hit everyone's eyes. A mighty sword, complete with a dyed blond lion's mane. No, it was too enormous to simply be called a sword.

I heard Albert mutter softly in English beside me.

"Oh, my God," he said.

"And thus, I have proven that I am a perfect being."

The guys who'd just borne witness couldn't even utter a sound.

"Are you even human?" said Sudou. That was all he could say in the face of a power so overwhelming, it crossed national borders.

If Sudou and Katsuragi were rifles and Albert was a bazooka, then Kouenji was a tank. Nobody could win against such overwhelming firepower. Its colossal size, armor, and destructive power would take down anyone in its path. There wasn't a single student in this massive bathhouse that could defeat Albert...which meant none of them who could stand up to Kouenji either.

Then, just as everyone was about to hand him the crown...

"Ha. Hold it, Kouenji."

A voice emerged from the vicinity of the tub that Kouenji had been in moments ago.

"R-Ryuuen...?" someone stammered.

Ryuuen, the former leader of Class D himself, was warming up in the whirlpool bath, near Kouenji. There was fire in his eyes. He must have been watching Albert and Kouenji's battle.

"You can't possibly think you're a match for me," Kouenji said.

"No. Not even I can win against that thing you're packin'. However, there might be at least one person here who could give you a good fight."

Everyone started looking around at each other as he said that, even though there was no way such a person could exist. Then I realized what he meant.

Ryuuen had caught me in his trap.

"Oh, ho? And *who* might that be?" asked Kouenji. His interest must have been piqued.

"Can't say. But if I'm not mistaken, there is still one person here covering himself up with a towel, hiding his true power."

Having dropped that bomb, Ryuuen entered the bath and turned his back to us. Fortunately, only a few people seemed to buy what he'd said...and yet, everyone's gazes were intensifying. Somehow, I felt like not just the current occupants of the bathhouse but people all throughout Japan were now paying attention.

"No way. A guy like you? No way, dude," said Yahiko, glaring at me.

"Are you really taking what he said at face value?" I asked.

"I don't intend to, but...it's kind of curious that you're the only one still covering yourself up all this time."

"Curious or not, I just never had any intention of joining this game." I took a step back.

"Okay, fine. But let us check, just in case."

Yamauchi and Yahiko approached, as though they

were trying to flank me. Ryuuen wore a smug smile on his face.

I'm gonna make you taste defeat.

That's what his look and smile said.

Just as I thought...

Ryuuen, who had no way of knowing what my member looked like, had intentionally set this up. He was intent on making me lose, one way or another. It was a malicious sort of attack, very much like Ryuuen.

I could use all my strength and bolt from the bathhouse, but then I'd have to forego bath time while here at the camp. Sooner or later, the veil would be lifted. I could try to turn the tables and punch out every student here, but that strategy was hardly worth consideration. Either way, I lost. There was no way I could avoid this incomprehensible battle anymore.

Kouenji, seeing I wasn't budging an inch, laughed.

"Ha ha ha! No need to feel embarrassed, Ayanokouji Boy. Even if you happen to be wearing *protection*, that's something a lot of Japanese children do. It's an important thing to protect."

"You're not protecting anything though, Kouenji."

"That's because I possess overwhelming strength, you see. I have no need for armor."

I had to get out of this. Think. Find a means of escape—

"You guys, do the chant. The chant."

Despite having dropped out of this competition himself, Ryuuen spurred everyone else on from where he sat in the bath, setting off another of his traps. He countered my strategy, ensuring I could no longer escape.

"Take it off! Take it off! Take it off!"

All the guys started chanting, calling for me to take it off. The identity of the person goading them on didn't matter one bit to them. I was trapped, all thanks to Ryuuen. And all I'd wanted was to wash away my fatigue after a tiring day...

"All right."

Sometimes, you just had to fight. I had no choice but to admit that now was one of those times. And as a man, if you had a weapon, you should wield it. Winning or losing didn't matter, and nor did pride.

"Fine, whatever."

"Do you want me to put you out of your misery, Ayanokouji? Read you your last rites?" asked Sudou. I waved him away.

Everyone kept calling for me to take it off, so I removed the towel wrapped around my hips, and then...

The chanting suddenly dropped. There was complete silence, as if the unruly noise earlier were just a dream.

"F-for real, dude? Ayanokouji, he..."

"I don't believe it..."

The guys spoke in whispers.

"Well, well. I'm honestly impressed, Ayanokouji Boy. To think there exists a Japanese person who can hold their own against me. Truly, a margin of a few millimeters might as well be nonexistent."

"It's like a showdown between two T-rexes..."

The guys looked on with admiration and exasperation.

"You are all living witnesses to history," said Kouenji, tossing his towel over his shoulder with a laugh. "However, victory is mine. If they are both T-rexes, as you put it, then the difference lies in the number of prey they've devoured. In other words: experience."

Without supplying any further details, Kouenji dipped back in the tub.

4.4

• •

IT WAS 1:00 A.M., well past lights-out, and I was lying awake in my bed. Everyone else was sleeping soundly. I should have been sleeping in order to prepare for tomorrow. That reason I was still awake lay in the single piece of paper beneath my pillow with the number 25 written on it.

The note's simplicity didn't leave much to the imagination. The memo represented 25:00—in other words, one o'clock in the morning. I didn't have any clue about who had put the note there, but I was awake now so I could find out. If it were just a simple prank or something completely different from what I was imagining, then, well, that would be that. I could just use this time to calm down and think about things.

What lay at the heart of this special exam? The bigger picture was slowly coming into view, bit by bit. Of course, this was all speculation, since we hadn't been told exactly how the test would be scored. But I did know for a fact that there were going to be several things included in this exam.

Zen.

We would be graded on everything from our manners at the start of *zazen* to the posture we held during it. If we behaved inappropriately or did anything that got us smacked by the zen stick, we'd probably have points docked for it.

Long-Distance Relay Race.

That sounded simple. A test of our speed.

Speech.

Every person in the large group would deliver a speech on four criteria, aforementioned. The grading system for this had already been disclosed.

Written Exam.

I expected this would focus on the subject of ethics. It sounded like it would be a standard essay-based test.

There were other things that concerned me, like "cleaning" and "cooking meals," but I couldn't determine how those would be scored yet. In some cases, things like tardiness or causing trouble might also be included in our assessments.

A lot of students were probably agonizing over how to approach this completely different special exam. A strategy, while vital, could only be devised once you understood something's true nature. The goal of this exam was ostensibly to make us work as a group, support each other, and earn a high average score. Simple, on the face of it.

But though it might sound easy at first, you could tell just from watching the groups be formed that this was going to be an uphill battle. It was extremely difficult for students who were normally hostile toward one another to truly cooperate. Horikita and Hirata, to speak of our own class, or Ichinose and Katsuragi, to speak of others, were probably focusing on encouraging such cooperation. Wielding influence within your group and having leadership skills made all the difference.

Selecting the members of your group was important, of course, but it was nearly impossible to tell right off the bat which students were capable of scoring well in this exam. Although Keisei's academic prowess was nothing to scoff at, and thus, he could be expected to do well in that regard, he seemed to struggle with even the two five-minute sets of *zazen* on the first day. Some students couldn't cross their legs at all.

It was still too early to tell whether academic or athletic skill would be a good measure of how students would do from here on out. Rather, it was the most adaptable students who were likely to come out on top.

Additionally, it was probable that more than a few students were opting to pursue strategies that deviated from the basic one of encouraging cooperation. I'd sensed when the rules were explained to us that even the school had struggled to prepare for this rather unorthodox special exam. This had been true of every special exam, of course, but there had always been loopholes in the rules to exploit. Blind spots that the school couldn't see. Such as how Ibuki and Horikita had traded blows back on the uninhabited island, even though violence was prohibited.

Of course, if you did happen to get caught committing breaking the rules, then the consequences would be huge. The majority of the students probably wouldn't risk it, with immediate expulsion at stake. Besides, the situation was far too complex for a mere rule violation to secure you a victory.

Could you find a barely existing blind spot, exploit a loophole, and take a shot that would somehow outdo the people following the traditional strategy? A high hurdle to overcome. I'd tried a lot of things in the special exams we'd had so far. On the uninhabited island, I had Horikita retire and switched up leaders. On the cruise ship, I had the trick with my phone. I purposefully drew attention to myself during the Sports Festival. And I shut Kushida down during the Paper Shuffle.

But this time, I'd decided not to take action. I would just sit and observe, continuing to collect information. I had determined that was what I had to do in order to fade into the background and graduate like any ordinary student. Even if that meant Class C took some hard blows this time around, I wouldn't do anything.

I also wanted to show Sakayanagi and Nagumo, who both had a certain degree of interest in me, that I had no intention of fighting...though I had my doubts about how well that would work. Horikita's brother couldn't really blame me for anything if all I did was observe. However, there was one measure I could take, and it was defense. If there were a student out there who was trying to get me expelled, then it was only natural that I would defend myself.

It was already past 25:00 now, and I had yet to see anything out of the ordinary. If that was the case, should I go back to sleep?

But just then, something happened.

The hallway door cracked open slightly and a little bit of light came through. It was Morse code. They were communicating via the flickering light. Since it was extremely dark in the hallways at night, several flashlights had been made readily available to us, and the person out there was probably using one. Light made no sound. The perfect way to signal me to come meet with them.

I got out of bed and silently stood. Our rooms weren't equipped with toilets. Getting up to go to the bathroom in the middle of the night was a perfectly natural thing to do.

4.5

• •

THE CORRIDOR WAS pitch-black, but I could tell someone was moving from the faint sound of footsteps. I followed that sound, and the person holding the light turned out to be Horikita Manabu.

"Huh, to think you'd contact me. Isn't that kind of conspicuous?" I asked.

In order for him to place a note on my bed, he'd have to know where I slept. In that case, there were only a couple people who might have helped him. It was probably either Ishikura or Tsunoda, the third-year students who'd played cards with Nagumo. They could have told Horikita which bed was mine.

"More than a few students meet in secret when others are fast asleep. There are probably two or three schemes being implemented during this exam, after all."

Everyone—first-, second-, and third-years alike—was pulling out all the stops in order to win. That being said, such clandestine meetings rarely led to anything good.

"Do you know why I called you here?"

"Because Nagumo is acting weird. I can't think of any other reason."

"Exactly. I thought you might have something on him, since you're in the same large group. Plus, I wanted to respond to the message you sent me back on the bus."

"I'll say this up front: prepare to be disappointed. There's no sign Nagumo is up to anything strange."

I was lying. There *were* several things about Nagumo's behavior that concerned me. He'd directly challenged the elder Horikita to a contest in front of a huge crowd of people, and losing that contest would be a pretty poor showing for the second-years. Both his upperclassmen and underclassmen would view him with skepticism in the future.

If you were going to do combat in public, you should do so only when you were sure the odds were in your favor. I didn't sense that was the case here. Since Horikita's brother had instructed Nagumo to fight fair and square, I'd expected Nagumo to be strict about making sure everyone in our large group paid attention to our lessons... but there was no sign of him doing anything of the sort.

That was probably making Horikita Manabu anxious.

If not, he wouldn't have taken the massive risk of contacting me like this.

"Then you think Nagumo is going forward without any kind of scheme?"

"Who knows? I think not involving any third parties really limits what you can actually do."

Even if you could remind people not to talk in class, doze off, or be late, that wasn't going to improve test scores by leaps and bounds. At most, it might avoid having points docked.

"Currently, our large group is more unified," Horikita's brother calmly assessed.

True, his group was mostly composed of Class A students, including those from the first year. Whatever the test was, there was a strong chance they'd win. That had to be why he felt anxious about Nagumo's inaction.

"What are the odds he'll go back on his word?" I said. "Maybe he wants to see you lose no matter what it takes."

"Nagumo shows no mercy to those who defy him. He's employed underhanded methods like Ryuuen more than once. He's also directly responsible for the second-years' unusually high expulsion rate. However, he's never once broken a promise."

"You believe he's serious about not involving any third parties?"

"Yes."

Horikita's brother nodded decisively. He and Nagumo had served together on the student council for nearly two years, and he must have seen how the other boy operated. I had my doubts, but hearing the certainty in his voice gave me that answer. An answer that applied not just to Horikita's brother, who was before me right now, but perhaps to all the second- and third-year students too.

After hearing those words of absolute certainty from him, I felt doubt at first, but then I had arrived at my answer. I could say that for Horikita's brother, who was in front of me right now, and perhaps for all of the second-year and third-year students as well.

I should give Horikita's brother some advice here and now. But it probably wouldn't do much good. He'd already determined that his best defense was to trust in his enemy's principles.

"This has been a waste of time, apparently," said Horikita's brother, turning his back to me. "Oh, to answer your earlier question... The student council can influence the special exams. The council is supposed to represent the students' perspectives and can therefore make significant revisions to penalties or meddle with the rules. However, the council cannot make these decisions on a whim."

"I see."

With that, Horikita left.

"He might lose," I muttered, unable to keep it in.

Well, perhaps that was the wrong word. Horikita's brother would make no mistakes. He would doubtlessly manage his group well. But even so, we clearly didn't fully understand this exam. It was possible this would drastically change the course of our third semester.

5

THE FIRST HALF OF THE GIRLS' BATTLE: ICHINOSE HONAMI

B Y THE TIME day three rolled around, it seemed like a lot of stuff had happened with the boys. But as a girl, I, Ichinose Honami, couldn't know the details.

Let's rewind to the day that the special exam started and tell the story from there.

"Now that we've formed our groups, let's do our best to get along, everyone!"

That was what I said to all the members of my group before bedtime. Despite the many twists and turns, ups and downs, and ongoing drama, at least I now knew the allies who'd be facing this exam by my side.

Wang Mei-Yu-san, Shiina Hiyori-san, Yabu Nanami-san, Yamashita Saki-san, Kinoshita Minori-san, Nishino Takeko-san, Manabe Shiho-san, Nishi Haruka-san,

Motodoi Chikako-san, Rokkaku Momoe-san, and I formed a group of eleven people. I was the only one from Class B, and there was also only one person from Class C. The rest were from Classes A and D. Manabe-san and Nishino-san seemed to be considered problem children even within their own class. In short, we were a group of oddballs.

I didn't know Mei-Yu-san well, and the remaining students who'd been brought in to fill the group didn't really know each other either. I needed to hurry up and build some relationships—fast.

"Let's do our best, Ichinose-san."

"Looking forward to working with you, Shiina-san. I've wanted to get to know you for a while."

"Is that so? That's an honor."

But as for Class C—no, they were Class D now—we hadn't really mingled with any of them at all. With Ryuuen-kun behind them, we could never get to a place where we could befriend them, no matter what we did. I supposed it was still unclear whether he really had stepped down or not, but since we'd finally put this group of girls together, I wanted us to get along.

The main thing we needed to avoid was someone being expelled if our group fell short. In other words, we needed to avoid someone invoking the solidarity rule and dragging another person down with them. Even if my first loyalty was to my comrades in Class B, now that we'd formed this group, I couldn't play favorites. That was what I had told myself.

Wang Mei-Yu-san wasn't actively participating. To be more precise, it felt like she *couldn't* participate even if she wanted to. It would be simple for me to lend a hand, but this group was mainly composed of girls from Class A and Class D, many of them ones with big egos. If I stuck my nose in where it didn't belong or tried to forcefully lead them along, they might decide they couldn't trust me.

So I decided to wait. If no one else took the initiative and started helping Wang Mei-Yu-san, I'd do something about it.

"Hey, you're Wang Mei-Yu-san, right?"

"Y-yes."

Shiina-san approached her, addressing her gently. Shiina-san had taken on the role of representative, even for a group like this. She was a really reliable person. I hadn't put myself forward for the role, partly because Shiina-san had volunteered right away, but also because I didn't think that we could really aim for the top spot with the members we had.

"This all must make you really nervous, huh? I mean, being surrounded by people you don't know."

"U-um, well, I wouldn't..."

"It's completely understandable if you're feeling bewildered, especially when you're surrounded by strangers and told to get along with them."

"Yeah. Exactly, Shiina-san."

You couldn't transform a group of strangers into friends just because you wanted to. It was the kind of thing that happened naturally or not at all. If you overthought it, you'd lose your footing and fail.

"Hey, Ichinose-san. Have you ever had a boyfriend?" asked a girl from Class A.

"Well... I'm embarrassed to say it, but no. I don't have any romantic experience."

"I see. Huh, you look like you'd be super popular, though. Maybe you're the type of girl who has really high standards or something."

"I don't really think I am, but...I dunno."

"Well, do you like any guys?"

"Huuuh?!"

The question was so sudden, I couldn't help but panic.

"There are rumors going around. People say they see you hanging around with Nagumo-senpai a lot, just the two of you..."

Well, it was certainly true that I'd been working a lot with President Nagumo after joining the student council.

I'd never imagined it would lead to rumors like this, though.

"Setting aside whether I like him or not, I'm really not even on the student council president's radar. He doesn't look at me that way."

"No way, that can't be."

"Yeah. I mean, you're *you*, Ichinose-san. It wouldn't be strange if you and Nagumo-senpai started going out."

"Either way, there isn't anyone I like now..."

"Wait, right now? So you *used* to like someone?"

The girls started to grow excited all at once. This was a dangerous topic if you misspoke.

"No, you got it all wrong. Well, I suppose there was this senpai I admired, but before I realized that I had a crush on him, he graduated..." I trailed off, trying frantically to deny it.

The girls all exchanged looks before bursting into laughter.

"What? What? Did I say something weird?" I asked.

"No. It's just, like, you're answering these questions all so seriously."

"Ichinose-san, you're way too honest. It's okay to just brush off stuff you don't want to answer, okay?"

"Does that mean you dodged the question yourself earlier, Chikako-chan?"

"Eek."

And so our girls' night gathering grew lively once more. How should I put it? It felt like we could talk forever and never get sleepy.

"Hey, I'm not gonna answer any questions I don't want to, okay?"

"Okay, then, how many times has someone confessed to you so far?"

"Huh? Um, three times. Well, if you're including preschool, four times. I think. And if I add in that one other time, then five."

"See, you *did* answer!"

"Nyaa!"

I was no good at talking about romantic stuff. I was so unfamiliar with anything of the sort, I was afraid I'd slip up and prove my ignorance.

"Hmm, I wonder. Could it be that Ichinose-san is the kind of person who's incapable of lying?"

"You may be right."

The girls were getting really fired up. It was probably better to deny that.

"That's not true. Really."

"Really?"

"For example, you might need to make a gamble or

two during the special exams, right? I might try to mislead someone in a situation like that."

"Then you're fine with telling lies."

"Hmm. I don't think that's quite right, either. I don't think anyone really *wants* to tell lies. The best way to put it might be... I try to tell the truth as much as possible. Well, that's not entirely right either. I guess I don't like telling lies to avoid hurting people..."

"Isn't that kinda weird, though? I mean, wouldn't you *want* to lie to avoid hurting people?"

"Yeah. I think lies told to avoid hurting people are definitely gentle, as lies go."

But...that wasn't really the case for me.

That was right. This was the ordeal I'd set for myself.

"I think a lie told to avoid hurting someone is just delaying the pain 'til later..."

A single lie could lead to something much, much worse down the road. I never wanted to go through that again. Those painful days. That cruel time.

CLASSROOM OF
THE ELITE

6 UBIQUITOUS THINGS

SUNDAY CAME AND WENT in a flash, and it was now Monday, the fifth day of the test. All four hours of our morning lessons were devoted to exercise. We had to walk or run an eighteen-kilometer course that was going to be used for the long-distance relay race, and then be back for our afternoon lessons. Since it was a relay race, each person would only be running a kilometer or two. But we were in the mountains, and the way could be rocky and steep.

We walked for about five kilometers, exhausting our stamina. The other day, we'd only worked up a light sweat. The difference between then and now was incredible.

"Seriously, how much higher does this slope go?! This is friggin' nuts, dude. This is way too hard," spat Ishizaki as we passed a sign telling us to be wary of wild boars.

He turned back toward me, with a look in his eye that suggested he'd spied something unpleasant. "Speaking of wild boars, are the ones here pretty big? Like this guy?"

"Truly amazing. I underestimated you, Ayanokouji."

Hashimoto and a bunch of other guys started complimenting me, which just made me extremely uncomfortable. Knowing they were going to use this joke to mess with me for a while was profoundly awkward. Albert even went so far to applaud.

But soon, they were out of time to tease me.

Even though the road that led to the summit was paved to allow vehicles, the incline was extremely steep. Simply walking up it was going to strain our legs. On top of that, since we'd been getting up early to make breakfast, we were more tired than the upperclassmen. We only got a break on Sunday because the school showed some mercy.

"How long is it gonna take for us to get back?"

"The average person's walking speed is four kilometers per hour. It's a distance of eighteen kilometers. If we walk the entire time, it'll take four and a half hours."

"You've gotta be screwing with me. We ain't gonna have any time left to eat lunch!"

"Then we have to run, Ishizaki. The more we run, the sooner it'll be over," said Class B's Moriyama, rather bitterly.

Though our whole large group had started out to-gether, most of the second-year and third-year students were moving faster than us.

"Don't talk crazy. No way in hell I can run eighteen kilometers."

"Don't tire yourself out by talking for no reason. We're all here because you agreed with my strategy, right?" warned Keisei, panting heavily as he spoke.

Students with decent stamina could have started to sprint right away, but doing that continuously for eighteen kilometers certainly wasn't the best idea. Keisei's strategy was that we would walk for the first nine kilometers until we reached the turnaround point and run from there. We'd mostly be going downhill by then, something that Keisei had factored into his proposal.

"We ain't even started runnin' yet. Like hell we'll be able to hold out until the turnaround point."

"Shut up... Just be quiet and walk."

Keisei wasn't very good with physical exertion. His legs must have been hurting him already, because his composure was starting to fray. With thirteen kilometers or so to go, we might not be able to make it back within the stipulated time. It was only natural to want to keep talking to a minimum and focus on walking.

That said, this exercise had made me begin to understand who the runners were. Yahiko and Keisei were definitely not suited to this task. Kouenji, who was lagging behind us, could probably be an asset to the group. But I doubted he'd take it seriously enough to run.

"Be quiet and walk, huh? You're actin' all high and mighty for someone who looks like a zombie, Yukimura."

Ishizaki kept at it. It didn't seem like there'd be any cutting back on the chatter.

"I'm saying this for the sake of the group, as the representative. Please don't talk."

"Oh, as the representative? Screw you."

Maybe because of all the stress he was under, Ishizaki just kept verbally assaulting Keisei. Moriyama and Tokitou from Class B couldn't let that slide.

"Enough, Ishizaki. Yukimura's right."

Sensing someone behind me was getting further away, I turned to find that Kouenji had veered off the byroad and gone into the forest. No one else had noticed. They were solely focused on looking ahead. Ishizaki wasn't our only problem child. I couldn't see Kouenji anymore and there wasn't any sign that he was coming back; this probably wasn't a minor detour.

"Well, it is what it is..."

I considered quietly chasing after Kouenji, but every-one might think I'd ditched too. So I spoke up.

"Kouenji went off on some other path back there. I'll go call him back."

"Huh? What in the hell is that weirdo doin'?!" With no students around who seemed capable of stopping him, Ishizaki's voice seemed to just get louder and louder.

"Don't let him distract you, Ishizaki. If you don't ig-nore Kouenji, you'll only be hurting yourself."

Keisei's strategy was to treat Kouenji as if he were invisible. A sound strategy, but ignoring him completely was easier said than done.

"Sorry, Kiyotaka. Can I leave this to you?" asked Keisei apologetically.

I could tell Keisei didn't have the energy to go back and look for Kouenji. I told him I'd do it.

"Hey, this is Kouenji we're talking about. Won't he be kind of a handful? Want me to help?" offered Hashimoto. However, I politely declined his offer.

"No matter who goes, we might not be able to bring him back. Getting as many people as possible to finish the run would look better to the school. I don't see how I could get lost on this route, anyway."

"You're probably right. Come back the moment you think it's a lost cause, though."

I nodded my assent and went in pursuit of Kouenji. I hadn't planned on actively making a move, but I wasn't often in a position to speak privately with Kouenji. If I was going to talk to him, this was probably my only chance.

6.1

THE NARROW PATH was just a dirt road. Despite the poor terrain, I picked up my pace. If Kouenji was on foot, I calculated I could catch up to him in a minute or two. However, he must have gone faster, because there was no sign of him.

"What a pain in the neck..."

Going faster was one thing, but running down a dirt road was troublesome. I increased my pace, looking for any tracks Kouenji might have left behind on foot. After a hundred or so meters, I finally spotted him up ahead.

As I looked at his back, I remembered a similar situation back on the island, when Airi had been there. Kouenji had left us in the dust back then too.

"Kouenji," I called, closing the distance between us.

"Oh, ho, if it isn't Ayanokouji Boy. This isn't the cor-rect route, is it?"

"I'm here to keep you from potentially getting expelled via the solidarity rule. Why did you take this detour?"

"I caught a glimpse of a wild boar. I dare say I was in-terested. So I gave chase."

That certainly wasn't what I'd expected to hear. I re-frained from asking what he planned to do if he found it.

"Rest easy. I shall return in time. It shouldn't take someone like me even thirty minutes," he added.

Looked like I had no choice but to trust him.

"Incidentally, do you have any other business with me?" asked Kouenji. He must have sensed something was up because I hadn't walked away.

"About the exam. I want you to help the group."

"I'm getting so tired of hearing people say that to me. I feel like my ears will start to bleed if I have to listen to those words just once more."

I didn't doubt Keisei and the others had been trying to persuade him when I wasn't around. And yet, Kouenji hadn't budged a single inch.

"You don't have to get an outstanding score. Just do what you're supposed to."

"You do not get to decide that. I do. You know that, don't you? I will see you later," said Kouenji, motioning that he was about to leave. But I grabbed his arm and stopped him.

He tried to take a step forward, leaving me no choice but to hold fast and dig in my heels. I expected him to resist, but for some reason Kouenji went slack.

"Heh. I see. So that's how it is then, Ayanokouji Boy," said Kouenji, turning toward me.

"What do you mean? What's how what is?"

"The person who tamed the Dragon Boy."

"Dragon...who?"

"I'm talking about that mischievous rascal, Ryuuen."

"What does Ryuuen have to do with me?"

"You're quite good at playing dumb. You don't let your intentions slip through at all when you feign indifference."

"I really don't understand how you arrived at this conclusion."

"Because of your touch on my arm. I can tell by the heat being transmitted through your skin."

I'd already figured Kouenji wasn't normal, but apparently he was even more of an eccentric than I was. He got all that from me grabbing his arm?

"Sorry, but this is a huge misunderstanding," I said.

"Really? Judging by the way Delinquent-kun looks at you and acts around you, and the reactions of all those around you, I would think it's a certifiable fact."

Kouenji didn't have a single shred of evidence, but he sounded overwhelmingly confident in his observations. It'd be pointless to attempt any further deception.

"Heh. Relax. I have no intention of revealing what you're keeping hidden. Even if you do happen to be exceptional in your own way, you're still a small fry to me. One of many. So, whether I'm right or wrong, there should be no problem as long as I don't spill the beans. Correct?"

"Well, I do want to clear up this misunderstanding."

"Too bad. That's not going to happen, Ayanokouji Boy. Even if you have third parties vouch for you, assuring me that you had nothing to do with any of it, my mind is made up. I'm certain of what I know."

"I see. Well, can we get back to the matter at hand?"

"You're talking about me doing my part as a member of the group, yes?"

"Can you?"

"I've said this repeatedly. I refuse."

He answered clearly and decisively.

"I will act in accordance with my own wishes. That is my philosophy. Will I take the exam, or won't I? What grade will I achieve? All of those things depend on how I feel in that moment."

"I see."

I had considered various means of persuasion, but haphazardly trying anything out here would probably backfire. I was going to have to leave things to chance, but there was a strong possibility that doing so would cause the least harm. It was clear as day that Kouenji wanted to avoid being punished with expulsion. I had no choice but to gamble on that.

There was nothing I could do for now but watch Kouenji walk away, chasing the wild boar.

"I don't think there's anyone in the world who can make that guy do anything."

It didn't matter if it was Horikita's brother, or Nagumo, or even his own classmates. Such was my honest impression of my classmate, whom I had known for about a year now.

. . . .

AFTER LEAVING KOUENJI, I returned to the course. Even though I'd been gone for less than ten minutes, I was probably in last place now. I didn't see any students from the group in front of or behind me, so I decided to rush a bit and catch up. A short while later, I sighted a group of first-year students—Keisei and the other guys. Tokitou noticed me first right away, and then everyone else looked over to me.

"Well, for the record, I did find him, but..."

"No dice, huh?"

Hashimoto, who predicted that would happen, wore a bitter smile on his face. The other students didn't blame me either and just groused about Kouenji's absence. Somehow or other, we eventually made it to the turnaround point, happily badmouthing Kouenji as we went. Chabashira was waiting for us there, arms crossed. I hadn't seen her in a few days, but it seemed she'd been tapped pretty regularly to help out with various lessons.

"The second-years and third-years have turned back. You guys are all that's left," she said.

"What time is it, sensei?"

"It's almost eleven o'clock now."

That meant we still had an hour to go until our lunch break. If this were a flat road, it wouldn't be too hard to make it back in time. However, we had already trudged nine kilometers up an incredibly steep, winding slope. Our stamina had been depleted considerably. If we didn't run at a solid pace, this exercise was going to take a bite out of our lunch break.

"I'm going on ahead. I don't want to be late for lunch."

"Wait. We'll be taking roll call before you head back down. Each person has to state their class and name."

A board was brought out, probably for the purposes of recorded students who'd made it to the turnaround point. Once Ishizaki signed, he turned on his heel and ran, leaving the group behind. Looked like it would be every man for himself, group be damned. Albert followed afterward.

"Let's go, Kiyotaka."

"You go on ahead. I'd like to wait and make sure Kouenji comes back."

"That's all well and good, but...we only have an hour left."

"I'm fast enough. Don't worry."

"Short-distance running and long-distance running are two different things, you know. Well, I guess I'm not really one to talk," said Keisei, letting out a self-derisive chuckle before running awkwardly.

"I'm going," said Hashimoto.

"Yep."

Hashimoto, the last member of our group, stretched and then ran off. Chabashira and I were the only two people left.

"It doesn't seem like you have anything you want to discuss with me," she said.

"I'm just waiting for Kouenji. If we don't get the tail end moving, it'll be trouble."

"Trouble?"

It wasn't really a big deal. If you had stamina to spare, like Ishizaki, who was quick to take the lead and clear the race, you'd never notice the students who gave up partway through. This wasn't a timed trial. We just had to clear the course by the set time; whether we did that in one hour or four didn't matter. Keisei didn't have much stamina himself, but it was obvious he was pushing himself hard to keep from holding us back.

About twenty minutes later, Kouenji finally showed up.

"This seems to be the turnaround."

He'd gotten around a bit, apparently. Traces of leaves and dirt were stuck to his jersey.

"You're the last one, Kouenji. You have forty minutes left."

"That seems to be the case. I wish I'd taken my time a bit more, but my encounter with the wild boar ended a bit sooner than expected."

"Wild boar?" asked Chabashira.

She clearly had questions about that particularly strange and sudden part of what he'd just said, but Kouenji turned around and ran off.

"Roll call, Kouenji. You'll be disqualified otherwise," said Chabashira.

"My name is Kouenji Rokusuke. Remember it well, *teacher*," said Kouenji, without even turning around. His boisterous laughter echoed down the hill.

"Is that okay, sensei? He didn't state his class."

"Well, he gave his name. Let's cut him some slack."

"All right. I'll be heading off myself."

I wondered how much time had passed. Coming up on the sign warning us about wild boars again, I saw two male students' backs. One of them was Keisei, about what I'd expected. Rather than having exhausted his stamina, though, he seemed to be leaning on another student, who was propping him up. It looked like his left leg was hurt.

The other student was Hashimoto, who, as I'd anticipated, had stayed back to help pull Keisei along. As I ran over to them, the situation became clear.

"Did you get a sprain?"

"Ayanokouji? Yeah, looks that way. I'm guessing his ankle was at its limit by the turnaround point," said Hashimoto, explaining on Keisei's behalf.

It had to be tough to support another person's weight, but he didn't seem to mind. He walked slowly, close to Keisei, and didn't seem displeased whatsoever.

"Ugh, I'm so pathetic. Why can't I even do something like this?"

Keisei seemed frustrated, but I could still tell he'd changed. The old Keisei had found it hard to comprehend physical sports or anything other than written exams; he'd thought a student's life and work centered on academics. This Keisei had stretched before resuming the downward trek, and he'd gone last for the same reason I had.

"I'll help too," I said.

Two would be better for this job than one. I went to the other side and supported Keisei.

"Wait. If you do this, you'll both be late for lunch," said Keisei.

"If we just abandon you, you'll start running, won't you? You'd hurt your leg even more. That would spell trouble for all of us when the final test comes around. If we can ease your injury just by missing out on one lunch break, that's a small price to pay. Right, Ayanokouji?"

"You're probably right about that."

"But…"

"It was just good timing that the two of us were running near you," I said. "Don't feel embarrassed."

Hashimoto corrected me. "Three of us, actually. Although, man, that Kouenji dude runs insanely fast, huh? Dude's a monster."

"I get the feeling he has limitless stamina. There's no doubt he's number one in our grade level." I wasn't flattering Kouenji, just being honest.

"Maybe his horrible personality saved us from being saddled with Kouenji in Class A. Being in a group with him has made it pretty clear that he's an inconvenience for Class C, rather than an asset."

It was true that if Kouenji ever utilized his full potential, he'd be a huge threat. I couldn't say he made a good secret weapon if he wouldn't cooperate, though.

In the end, it was around 12:40 by the time we got back to camp, carrying the injured Keisei between us. After we arrived, Keisei got medical treatment at the infirmary. Hashimoto and I waited for him in the corridor. About ten minutes later, Keisei returned.

"How is it?" asked Hashimoto. Keisei smiled bitterly.

"It's just a light sprain. Thanks to the two of you, it ended up being a minor injury."

While he was favoring his left leg a bit, it did seem like he was walking pretty normally.

"There's not much time until the exam. Don't let it get any worse," said Hashimoto, lightly patting Keisei on the shoulder.

"Hey, I know you helped me out, but..." said Keisei. Hashimoto immediately understood.

"Don't worry about it. We'll keep this between us. That'll be more convenient, right?"

He'd gotten what Keisei was trying to say without having to hear it put in words. Keisei patted his chest and let out a sigh of relief.

6.3

● ●

SINCE I MISSED LUNCH, I was more excited than usual for dinner. After nabbing my seat, I immediately started eating.

"Hey, Kiyopon, the seat next to you free?"

That was Haruka's voice. When I turned around, I saw that all of the members of the Ayanokouji Group were together.

"Sheesh, Kiyopon. We've had a hard time trying to find you these past few days. You've been in weirdly difficult places to spot."

"Sorry. I guess I just don't know what to do in a cafeteria this huge."

Because of the way the groups were set up, it wasn't that easy to get the usual crew together. Since there weren't enough seats here, we moved a bit to find a spot where all five of us could sit.

"I-It's certainly been a while, hasn't it, Kiyotaka-kun?" said Airi bashfully.

It certainly was unusual for us not to talk for almost a full week. Even during the long holidays, we'd call or meet up.

"More importantly, you doing okay, Miyacchi? You're with Ryuuen, right?" Haruka asked, directing her question at Akito. She must have heard about that from somewhere.

"Well, I guess. I'm keeping my guard up, but it doesn't seem there's been any change. He's actually taking the classes seriously and participating."

"Like, even *zazen* and the relay?"

"Yeah. He's acting so normal, it's almost scary. If anything, he's handling himself way better than the awkward guys. It's just, well, I've tried talking to him a few times, but he doesn't seem to want to hang out with anyone."

"Maybe he kind of went crazy from the shock of losing a fight?"

"I dunno. I think this is just the way he's always been."

Akito braced himself, as if saying that he couldn't drop his guard.

"Anyway, how about you? Are you getting along well with your group?"

"Not much to say, personally. I'm not close with anyone in it, but I'm not fighting with anyone either. Airi and I are in the same group, so I'm good."

"I'm really glad that Haruka-chan is there for me."

So Haruka and Airi were in the same group? It must be reassuring to have even one close friend with you.

"It seems like our group has the most problems, Kiyotaka."

"You might be right about that."

"Really?"

Haruka and Airi exchanged looks, like this was the first they were hearing about it.

"Well, Kouenji won't follow orders, and Ishizaki snaps at people at the drop of a hat. Maybe it's because he has Albert with him, but we can't control him either. They're a pain in the neck."

"So Kouenji-kun is with you too... Are you all right, Kiyotaka-kun?"

"He's not actively harming us or anything."

"If anything, I'd say Ishizaki's the real problem child. Maybe he's gotten carried away since Ryuuen-kun was defeated. Not so long ago, he was just a lackey."

To tell the truth, I felt like one of the main reasons for Ishizaki's bad behavior was being put in the same group as me. I imagined feeling all this anger and frustration that he had no outlet for was causing him to lash out at anyone who wasn't me.

"In any case, I have to work hard as the representative," said Keisei. Even with the metaphorical equivalent of a bomb strapped to his leg, he kept doing his best to unite the group.

"You boys sure have it rough, huh?"

"S-somehow, I feel like we're kind of out of place."

"Come on, it's all right. I mean, if you girls are doing okay, that puts us at ease. Right?" said Akito.

True enough. Even with Kei funneling me information on the girls, there were still plenty of areas I couldn't see. If Haruka and Airi were together and moving along without issue, we boys could focus more on ourselves.

6.4

. . . .

IT WAS NOW the sixth day, Tuesday. On that day, I started to hear something a little odd from the guys.

They missed the opposite sex.

That was the current topic of conversation. I got the feeling that most of them were looking forward to dinnertime. While being surrounded by guys made me feel more relaxed, it wasn't exactly as fun.

"Agh, goddamn it. I feel like I'm losin' my mind being around guys all the time."

"If I were at an all-guys' school, I'd be dead, man."

Those were just some of the opinions I heard.

"Dude, havin' only guys around *stinks*. Like, literally."

I supposed it was inevitable that they were buying into the cliché that all guys had bad hygiene. The truth, however, was that there weren't many sweaty or smelly people here. They should be thankful this wasn't summertime. And, well...personally, I felt more relaxed being around only guys. That fact bore repeating.

"Ow, my hip..."

While we were in the middle of dusting, Keisei yelped in pain and crouched down. We had cleaning and breakfast duty to deal with every day, regardless of the lessons that continued at the same time, and we'd reached the point where you could see the weaker students starting to hit their limits. Keisei was complaining about his pain.

The area we'd been assigned to clean today was pretty big, forcing everyone in our group, which was already short-staffed to begin with, to work harder than usual. When even one person got injured, you had to make up for it.

"Whaddya mean, your hips hurt? Do your job."

Ishizaki grabbed Keisei's arm and forcefully yanked him up.

"I-I know. I'll do the work. Let go."

"Then do it right," spat Ishizaki, before heading back.

Keisei immediately tried to resume cleaning, but he just wasn't moving well. His sprained leg in particular was clearly stiff.

"Ugh."

He grunted quietly. He seemed to be enduring the pain, but if he pushed himself too hard, it'd affect him tomorrow.

"Grab a breather. I'll take your spot." There was no helping it. I'd clean Keisei's section for him.

"Sorry, Kiyotaka."

"Hey, we help each other out when we're in trouble." Problem solved.

Until...

"Hey. You *just said* you'd do it yourself!" said Ishizaki.

Apparently he didn't like that I was lending Keisei a hand. But he still made sure not to meet my eyes.

"I'll handle it," I replied.

Ishizaki didn't seem satisfied. He looked right through me, continuing to rain harsh words on Keisei.

"You're the representative, ain't you? Don't bitch about somethin' like cleaning."

"I get it."

Keisei felt responsible. When pressed, he'd fold.

"You don't *get* it. You're tryin' to push your job onto someone else right now, aren't you? I don't like that. Do it yourself."

"...I get it. I'll do it."

"All right then, there you have it. Do *not*, under any circumstance, give him a hand, Ayanokouji."

Ishizaki spoke to me for the first time, then immediately backed away, as if he was making his escape.

"Even if Keisei injures himself as a result?" I asked.

"If he gets injured, that's that," answered Ishizaki.

Apparently, Ishizaki wouldn't permit any attempt to help Keisei, even though he knew it wasn't good for the group. Albert silently approached Ishizaki, looking as though he was trying to tell him something. But Ishizaki didn't seem to be listening.

"Sorry, Kiyotaka. Guess I have no choice but to hang in there."

Keisei probably feared the group's mood would worsen if he didn't keep working. Ishizaki was already riled by Keisei's attitude over the past few days; he probably couldn't stand Keisei having someone else helping him out. Keisei understood that, which was precisely because he took Ishizaki's warning to heart and decided to do the job himself.

Still, if Keisei pushed himself too hard, we might pay for it later. Even if he held out today, there was no telling what tomorrow would bring. The actual exam included multiple physically demanding tests, like *zazen* and the long-distance relay. He might suffer even more than he did now. I wanted to make Ishizaki understand, but I doubted it'd be simple.

"Hey, Ishizaki. You're taking this a little too far," said Yahiko, unable to just sit back and watch the situation play out.

"It's his own fault for not being able to clean properly," said Ishizaki.

"I know that. But what about *him*? Go warn him too." Yahiko pointed at Kouenji, who had never once cleaned anything at all.

"I can't even communicate with that dude in Japanese. I ain't got time to persuade a gorilla," replied Ishizaki.

It wasn't as though Ishizaki hadn't warned Kouenji at least once before. He'd confronted him many times, to no avail, and given up. In that sense, you could say that the difference between Keisei and Kouenji was that Ishizaki was able to have an actual conversation with Keisei.

"If you have a problem, then you try and argue with him. It'll just be a waste of time, though."

"Fine. If I have to go, I'll go," said Yahiko, grabbing a broom and walking over to Kouenji.

"It's pointless. You'll see."

Ishizaki gave a derisive snort. Yahiko thrust the broom at Kouenji, trying to press him to clean. But after a few minutes, he walked away, totally exhausted. We might be in the same group, but we were all still enemies. Clearly, that hadn't changed.

Most of the students probably wanted this group activity to end as soon as possible. But the important thing to remember was that not every group was like ours. Even if it was only on the surface for now, some groups had to have members who were deepening ties with one another, forming real friendships and alliances, as if they were actually classmates. It wasn't just the first-years either. The same phenomenon could be observed among the upperclassmen who had managed to stabilize the relationships between their classes. They understood that everyone benefited if they cooperated.

Some students could plan ahead, while others were slaves to their darker impulses. Without a drastic gulf in skill to shake things up, it wasn't difficult to imagine the outcome of this battle.

"Aagh! I don't wanna do this! This is just *so friggin' dumb!* Why do we even gotta play nice? Pretend like we're friends with dudes from the other classes? Right, Albert?"

Albert didn't agree or disagree, but Ishizaki continued.

"Seriously, dude. I hate this group so friggin' much, I could die. There's that gorilla Kouenji, and the annoying loudmouth Yukimura who talks a big game even though he can't even run a friggin' marathon. Then there's those Class B dudes who just smile and laugh without a care in the world, and those do-nothin' Class A jerks. Idiotic."

WHACK! Ishizaki kicked the broom.

"You're free to curse us all you want, but keep cleaning."

"Shut up. Kouenji ain't doin' nothin', so why do I gotta?"

"Then you have no right to say anything to Yukimura, do you?" said Hashimoto.

But Ishizaki wasn't listening. He abandoned his cleaning duties and left, muttering something about going to the bathroom. Keisei bit his lip, frustrated.

"Keisei, you need to stop trying to shoulder everything alone. You can't change anything in the one or two days we have left. If you make an error in judgment now, you might regret it later," I said, giving Keisei some advice...or rather, hoping to confirm that he understood me.

"I understand, but there's nothing else I can do. If I lean on someone else for help, Ishizaki will just alienate the rest of the group even further. If I do nothing, it's highly likely that our group will come in last place. So I have to do something, even if it's reckless."

If the two options Keisei had just listed *were* the only options available, then acting recklessly probably would be the better choice. If you had no other paths to take, you just had to forge a new one for yourself. But Keisei didn't seem capable of forging anything right now, let alone a whole new option.

We needed someone who was capable of both understanding the group and also taking action for the sake of
others. I looked over at Hashimoto, who was quietly continuing to clean. He'd stopped Ishizaki from snapping at
Kouenji on the second day, and he'd responded perfectly
to the situation during the marathon practice. I had the
impression he could to hold the group together firmly, at
the right distance.

It was unclear how much Sakayanagi and Katsuragi
valued him, but I imagined he was a highly capable man—
if I evaluated him as a hypothetical enemy, anyway. He
was harder to read than the aggressive Sakayanagi and
the conservative Katsuragi, which made him a tougher
opponent.

"Look, just don't forget that I'm here. If you're in trouble, I'll help."

"Thank you, Kiyotaka. Just hearing you say that puts
me at ease."

If those words helped Keisei, I was happy to say them.

6.5

DURING OUR NEXT CLASS, it was clear the situation in our group had not improved. Keisei, feeling responsible, couldn't successfully give orders as the representative, and Ishizaki wouldn't even talk to anyone except Albert anymore. Even during mealtime, the only period when it was possible to create some kind of peace and harmony, our group never came together.

I decided to forget about them for the time being. There was nothing I could do for this group, anyway. I could give some advice to the struggling Keisei and the belligerent Ishizaki, but I had no intention of taking any direct action to help. Getting in deeper would defeat the purpose of trying to fade into the background.

Remembering Haruka and Airi, I decided to investigate what was going on with the girls again. However, it wasn't like I could just keep directly contacting Kei over and over again. She had responsibilities of her own, and if I kept contacting her, it might cause others to have their suspicions about the nature of our relationship.

Besides, the information I wanted wasn't related to the first-years. I wanted information on the second- and third- years. I needed to confirm Nagumo's true intentions toward Horikita's brother.

This meant my number of helpful contacts was very limited indeed. I took a small risk for that reason, attempting to contact Kiriyama by leaving a clue for him to find...but Kiriyama was in Nagumo's group. Even if he resented Nagumo, he probably couldn't help me this time.

I had to attack from a direction Nagumo didn't expect. One person came to mind. I had Kei investigate a certain second-year girl for me.

That person was named Asahina Nazuna.

She was in Class A, alongside Nagumo Miyabi, and was personally quite close with him. I'd seen Asahina eating meals with her friends in the cafeteria many times. Even now, I was monitoring her movements from afar. She wasn't on the student council but had a relatively high level of influence within her class. She also seemed to have a lot of influence over Nagumo.

There were other guys and girls who were close to Nagumo, but I chose Asahina for two reasons. The first was that, contrary to her rough exterior and way of speaking, she had a reputation for being dutiful and conscientious. She also didn't worship Nagumo.

The other reason was that the two of us had just so happened to bump into one another by accident. The difficulty in trying to dig up information on Nagumo came from the fact that virtually every single second-year supported him. If I clumsily attempted to make contact, I ran the risk of exposing information about myself instead.

I had to narrow my possible contacts down to someone who was least likely to leak information. This made our "accidental" meeting a powerful weapon. Information that only I know. Information that only Asahina could understand. I would use what that accident had birthed.

What accident do I mean? Well, it came from a good luck charm.

Asahina had accidentally lost it a while back, and I had just so happened to pick it up. At the time, I'd returned it without thinking much of it. To my surprise, though, the item was apparently very important to her. I could tell because she had brought it with her even to this camp. She always wore it on her person, with great care.

An accidental connection can sometimes be stronger than one created intentionally. Taking advantage of that connection, I wanted to ascertain whether or not she could be a useful source of information regarding Nagumo. The very circumstances of this camp made contacting her easy. All that remained was how to change our indirect connection into a direct one.

If I openly approached Asahina, then someone—even if it wasn't Asahina herself—might report it back to Nagumo. I wanted to avoid that. I'd been waiting for the right time, but Asahina spent almost all of her dinner hours with other people. I couldn't find a chance to be alone with her.

But today, that golden opportunity finally presented itself.

"I'm going to the bathroom. Be right back."

Just like that, Asahina got up, mid-meal. No other students accompanied her as she left, which was strange for a girl. I quickly followed her. I couldn't bother her while she was in the bathroom, so I patiently waited for her to come back out.

We'd probably have five minutes to talk at most. If I took up much more of her time, she might grow annoyed. I had no idea how much I could get done within those five minutes, but I had to remind her that we'd met earlier by chance. Emphasis on *chance*.

Soon, Asahina exited the bathroom. As usual, she was wearing her charm on her left wrist.

I pretended to be passing by.

"Hmm?" I muttered, quietly enough that Asahina might have thought I was just saying that to myself or that I was calling out to her.

When I said that, Asahina turned around. If I didn't respond quickly, she would probably think I'd been talking to myself and keep on walking. I decided to act.

"Oh, sorry. I was just thinking I'd seen that charm before. Please don't mind me," I said, motioning as if to continue walking. If she didn't respond, I was prepared to start a conversation myself.

"They don't sell this charm at the school anymore, though," she replied.

But she *did* reply, so without hesitating, I kept the conversation going.

"Oh, that so? Did you happen to drop it a while back, by any chance?" I asked. She should understand what I meant right away.

"Wait, are you...the person who found my charm?" she asked.

"Maybe... I picked it up on my way back to the dorm, uh...when was that, again?" I replied, pretending not to remember.

"No, I think I'm right. I see. So it was you," said Asahina, smiling happily. She drew nearer. "Thank you. When I realized I'd lost it, I was so upset. Ever since then, I've been scared I'll lose it again, so I've been wearing it more often."

She looked bashfully at her wrist.

"This charm, well, I bought it after I started school. It's not like I have any strong attachment to it in itself or anything. It's just...how do I put it? It's like emotional support. When I have it at hand, I just feel safer, you know? When I lose it, I get all anxious that something bad is going to happen, like it's a bad omen or something. I was so relieved that someone found it."

Well, bringing good luck *was* essentially a charm's purpose.

"I never imagined you'd be the one who found it."

"Do you know me?" I asked.

"Yeah, I know about you. You got a lot of attention in that relay race against Horikita-senpai. Oh, and Miyabi. Wait, you might not know his first name. Student Council President Nagumo talked to you a while back, right?"

"Wait. Were you there too?" I asked.

Of course, I knew the answer to that. Ichinose had also been present.

"Well, yeah."

Asahina seemed like the person who'd put up her guard if I told her I knew she'd been there, so I pretended not to remember. Just like picking up her charm, this meeting, where we just happened to cross paths, had to be accidental too.

"I'm pretty fast, but to be honest I don't really have anything else going for me. Maybe I've caught President Nagumo's eye through some kind of misunderstanding," I told her, making my voice sound troubled. Asahina nodded back repeatedly, showing that she understood.

"Nagumo really respects Horikita-senpai. Or, like, he's made Horikita-senpai a sort of goal. I think he was probably jealous that he didn't get to challenge him during the relay."

I couldn't sense any ulterior motive in Asahina's words. For better or worse, she seemed the honest type. I decided to step things up a bit.

"How can I get Nagumo-senpai to stop paying attention to me?" I asked.

"Well, how about you beat him at something? You could cut that smug Miyabi down to size. Personally, I'd love to see him lose for once," she replied, chuckling. She was probably joking, but I pretended to take what she said at face value.

"I see. That might be one option," I replied.

Asahina's eyes immediately darted back to me, an awestruck look on her face. Then a few seconds after, she burst into laughter.

"Ah ha ha ha! Come on, I was joking. Couldn't you tell?" she asked, laughing almost to the point of tears, lightly smacking me on the shoulder.

"So if Nagumo's ever defeated, that would be trouble, huh?" I said.

Just in case she still thought I was joking, I decided to strengthen my tone. If Asahina was the type of person who would pull back and report to Nagumo now, then this was the end of the line. Even if she reported back to him, it'd end with her thinking that I was just some uppity first-year.

"Wait, are you serious?" she asked.

"So you were joking, senpai?" I replied.

"Hey, look. This isn't something a first-year can do anything about," she replied, apologizing for joking around. But I continued speaking in the same tone.

"Among all the second-years I've met until now, you seem to be the most straightforward one, Asahina-senpai."

"The most straightforward?"

"It's hard to get any information from the second-years, outside of 'Nagumo Miyabi rules us all.'"

"That's some dangerous talk. I'm a second-year too, you know. Miyabi and I have a pretty deep relationship, understand?" she replied.

"It's not about being shallow or deep. What matters is how much you've been influenced by him."

Since they were in the same class, they couldn't be enemies, not truly. No matter what Asahina privately thought of Nagumo, she wouldn't want her class to suffer for it.

"I think those are similar things, though," she said.

"In that case, think of this as nonsense from a first-year." I bowed. "Please excuse me."

"Ah, wait. Somehow, I feel like I'm the bad guy here," she replied, releasing a deep sigh. Her smile disappeared. "I see you're not joking around. As an apology, please let me repay you for picking up my charm. If there's anything you'd like to know, I'll tell you."

"Are you sure? It might be seen as rebelling against Nagumo-senpai, you know."

"To be honest, I don't think anything drastic will happen just because I talk to you," she replied.

She seemed to be certain that telling me something about what was going on with the second-years wouldn't have a major impact. In other words, anything she told me would be information that didn't matter, even if it was leaked.

"Out of the girls in your grade level, how many would you say are especially close with Nagumo-senpai?" I asked.

"Girls who are close with him? Like, all of them. They trust Miyabi more than other guys, y'know."

I already knew he was no ordinary opponent, but this was an extraordinarily broad range of skills.

"What about the people who act as Nagumo-senpai's eyes and ears?" I asked.

"You really think I'd tell you that?"

"Well, as a senpai, it's okay to help a first-year out a bit, right?"

"Wow, you're cheeky," she replied, laughing. She didn't seem upset, though. "Well, if I do say so myself, the second-years have a really strong sense of unity. Honestly, we were more successful at dividing into groups than the first- and the third-years, you know? After they explained the test to us back on the bus, Miyabi said to immediately share that information with the other classes."

As I'd suspected—though they'd started out as enemies, the four second-year classes seemed on the way to becoming actual allies. Asahina told me the names of the four class representatives. The four classes kept in contact with one another and had even discussed the formation of their small groups with each other, to a certain degree. Apparently things had gone similarly for the girls.

"What about when you met up with the first- and third-year groups? Did you decide things randomly then too?"

Nagumo had proposed a draft selection system, which the first-year guys had carried out.

"For the most part, yeah."

"For the most part. So something was different?"

Asahina crossed her arms, appearing deep in thought.

"Why do you ask?"

I could tell Asahina was starting to have doubts. The silence lingered.

"Are you not going to tell me?" I asked.

"No, I will. It's just...when we were deciding on the large groups, some of the second-year girls made a small request. Or more like...they wanted some adjustments. At that time, the small group was made up of members that Miyabi could count on."

If the group formed based on Nagumo's orders, then he'd likely given them a special role. You wouldn't think that unless you knew what was going on within the second-years. From an outsider's perspective, it would simply look like friends coming together.

"Are there any first- or third-years who were selected to join that girls' large group that stand out in particular?"

"Even if you ask me that, I hardly know anything about the first-years. From the third-years, I guess there's

Tachibana-senpai, who was Horikita-senpai's secretary. Ah, but their representative is a different person, though. Miyabi said nothing weird would happen. He said he was going to do this fair and square."

"You have a lot of faith in Nagumo-senpai, huh?"

Horikita's brother also seemed to place a certain degree of trust in what Nagumo said. If I were to believe him and Asahina, then this line of reasoning might be considered a feint. Nagumo had promised to fight fair and square, but at the same time, he was making us jump at shadows. We feared he might be up to something behind the scenes, and he was using that to break our concentration.

"He always sticks to his word. He won't use dirty tricks. Besides, even if that group of girls does try to lay some kind of trap, it won't have any effect on Horikita-senpai and Miyabi's fight."

"That's right. It would be completely irrelevant."

Asahina was spot-on. Nagumo had proposed that only his group and Horikita's brother's group compete. The girls had nothing to do with it. Even if some of the second-year girls who were close with Nagumo happened to be in Tachibana's large group, it was irrelevant.

So was he making it look like he had something underhanded going on, while actually fighting above the board?

That would mean the seemingly meaningful words he'd uttered when he met up with the third-year student from his group, Ishikura-senpai, were just a fake-out too.

I supposed that if you were investigating him normally, you'd get the sense that these clues were popping up and then disappearing all over the place. An interesting way of doing things. This was different from Sakayanagi and Ryuuen: a unique strategy.

"What I can tell you, I suppose, is that whoever cares too much is the one who loses."

"You were a big help," I said.

I was grateful to Asahina for humoring my unreasonable request to discuss her class's internal affairs. Of course, she'd probably done so because she didn't think I could be an obstacle for Miyabi. She couldn't even imagine me being his opponent.

"Well, do your best to try and give Miyabi a run for his money, boy," Asahina. "I'll be rooting for you, even if it's only a little bit."

"Oh, just one more thing..."

"Hmm?"

If I combined what I'd just learned with the information I got from Kei, my understanding of the situation was becoming much clearer. I decided to push a little harder.

6.6

ON THE NIGHT of the sixth day, a sour mood hung over the entire group. If we let the day end like this, the group might fall apart entirely tomorrow. These rancor between us would just continue to intensify, making it all the harder to secure a high score on the test that was now just two days away.

Returning to the room after my bath, I found the atmosphere tense as ever. Ishizaki had walled himself off and was now refusing to speak to anyone else. Keisei, blaming himself, had fallen silent and retreated inward too. The Class B students kept trying to chat in an attempt to liven things up, but the awkward atmosphere was too much for them to bear, and they eventually went silent.

Eventually, after confirming that it was getting close to lights-out time, Yahiko flipped the switch and sent the room into darkness, seeking to bring this day to a merciful end.

"Hey, Ishizaki. You got a minute?" Hashimoto broke the long silence as we sat in the pitch darkness.

"No," replied Ishizaki.

Judging from the sound of rustling sheets that followed, he'd probably turned his back to Hashimoto, refusing to engage.

"At this rate, our group will be in extreme danger. We have the advantage of our team not being too big, but that also disadvantages us when it comes to the exam itself. In the worst-case scenario, Yukimura and someone else will be expelled," said Hashimoto.

You're going to be the one who goes down with him when that happens, Ishizaki. You know that? was the unsaid implication.

"Shut it. Even if I get expelled, whatever. I don't care. Shit happens."

"Dude, come on..." Hashimoto sighed deeply, as if giving up, at this refusal of his helping hand.

I couldn't see Hashimoto's face in the darkness. Had we passed the point of no return when it came to our group's unity? Maybe it was time we gave up.

"I played soccer in elementary school and junior high. Our school was pretty prestigious, so our team competed in national championships each year. I wasn't an ace player or anything, but I played in most games and did pretty well," said Hashimoto. He didn't direct the words to any one person in particular but addressed the room as a whole.

"Wait, you're not part of the soccer team now though, are you? It doesn't look like you got injured or anything," Yahiko pointed out, his voice cutting through the dark.

"No, I'm not. I know it's not really popular these days, but I used to smoke."

"So they found you out and kicked you out of soccer?"

"No. I hid my smoking habit well. Only my family knew."

"Even if smoking is disgusting, it's not a reason to quit soccer."

Yahiko's doubts were justified. If no one had known, then it couldn't have been an issue.

"I guess I just felt this sense of alienation or something. Everyone else would be working together to win the national championships, and part of me would just kind of observe them coldly. I knew I didn't belong. Also, I didn't really like soccer all that much. I decided to quit playing and just focus on my studies. I was pretty smart to begin with, so it wasn't that hard to keep getting good grades."

"What, now you're bragging? I ain't listenin' to this," interjected Ishizaki nastily.

"For better or worse, my only saving grace was that I could do reasonably well out in the world, I suppose. But there are still times when I feel regret. Whenever I see Hirata and Shibata practicing out on the field, I think it could have been me out there. Even though I didn't even like it that much. Strange, huh?" said Hashimoto.

He chuckled self-deprecatingly to himself. "What about you? What was your childhood like, Ishizaki?" asked Hashimoto.

"Huh? Why you askin'?"

"No reason."

"Hmph. Well, I ain't got anything to say." Ishizaki refused, to no one's shock.

Keisei opened his mouth, the next to join our conversation in the darkness.

"Ever since I was little, all I ever did was study. Maybe I was influenced by my older sister. She was a lot older than me, and she wanted to be a teacher, which meant I always had to play the role of the student. My sister was pretty ridiculous. She was always giving me these stupidly difficult problems to solve, even when I was in elementary school."

"So that's why you're so good at studying, huh?" replied

Hashimoto, responding as though he were trying to draw out the conversation.

"Yeah. And on top of that, I'm terrible at sports. No matter what I did, I generally came in near last place, just barely squeaking by. I decided to just focus on developing my strengths rather than conquering my weaknesses. I used to think there was no point in training your body if you weren't planning to become a professional athlete. Enrolling in this school made me begin to doubt that for the first time...but I still believed that I could study hard and be considered an appropriate pick for Class A," said Keisei.

He stopped speaking for a moment, as if he were remembering that time. Being put in Class D must have caused him immense despair.

"But then all these things I couldn't accept just kept happening. I don't agree with the solidarity system, and living on the deserted island made even less sense to me... In my own class, Sudou was like the polar opposite of me. He was great at sports, but he couldn't study. At first, I thought I'd been saddled with some ridiculous baggage. But on the uninhabited island and during the Sports Festival, Sudou's skills were far more useful than mine. I could see him shine, right beside me."

There was a hint of regret in his voice.

"There's still a part of me that can't accept it, to be honest. But I'm slowly beginning to realize that if all you can do is study, or all you can do is sports, then that's no good. That's the thing about this exam. If you can't do *both* of those things, then you can't score high. Am I wrong? Ishizaki?"

"Seriously, are you askin' me—?"

"I feel completely humiliated. Just like back on the uninhabited island and during the Sports Festival. I'm dragging the group down. I hurt myself, which has meant being a burden on others, and more importantly, I dragged down the group's morale. I have absolutely nothing to show Ishizaki, who, despite his complaints, has been contributing to the group just as much if not more than the average."

Ishizaki seemed about to mock him, but then he swallowed his swords. I couldn't see his face. But it was precisely because we were in the darkness, unable to see each other, that we could be this vulnerable.

"I'm sorry, Ishizaki... I'm sorry that your representative, who should be setting an example for the rest of you, is in this condition."

I could tell Keisei was trying to hold back tears. None of us were insensitive enough to cut in and say something. These were bitter tears.

"Stop screwing around. Why are you apologizing? I mean, I'm the one who blamed you," said Ishizaki. He let loose a chuckle, seemingly aimed at himself, before continuing on. "I mean, you were the one who agreed to be representative when no one else was willin'."

Even if we'd tried to push the role on Keisei, he could have refused it. As a matter of fact, Ishizaki had done so himself. He probably realized the good faith gesture Keisei had made by accepting the role now.

"It pissed me off, gettin' ordered around by you. But if you didn't give those orders, our group probably would've been way worse off. For makin' breakfast, and for the marathon."

"No doubts there," said Hashimoto, laughing.

Some students do well in academics, and some don't. Some excel in sports, and some struggle. When all these different students, with their own interests and backgrounds, come together to form a single class or group, they bring their problems with them. All the friendships and rivalries and everything of the sort.

Yahiko and the other students started chatting themselves, speaking up little by little.

That was the first night we started to feel like a real group.

7

WHAT IS LOST, WHAT ISN'T

IT WAS EARLY in the morning on the seventh day. The last full day. The final test would be held the next morning. Although Hashimoto's quick thinking had kept our group from collapsing, the alliances we'd slowly developed as we came together would end with that test. There were probably more than a few people here who felt a hint of reluctance to part ways.

At the end of the day, despite their dislike for Kouenji, I thought most of the students in our group were getting along well. Well, Ishizaki probably hated me even more than he did Kouenji, but he was doing his best not to let that show. He probably wanted nothing more than to confront me but knew exactly what would happen if he tried it.

Ishizaki was like Sudou, in that they were both quick to lose their tempers and had a coarse way of speaking. However, Ishizaki was cannier than Sudou. I also got the impression that he respected his opponents and earnestly acknowledged their strengths. That was probably why Ryuuen had kept him close.

That didn't mean Sudou was inferior to Ishizaki. He was more athletic by far, and at this point in time, probably doing better than Ishizaki academically too. As long as Horikita was helping him, Sudou would probably continue to improve. He and Ishizaki might be similar, but they had different weapons at their disposal.

"I want to talk about the long-distance relay tomorrow. Please hear me out."

Everyone, still in their beds, looked over at Keisei.

"There's only ten of us, so each person will be shouldering quite a bit of responsibility. But depending on how things play out, we might be able to turn this to our advantage."

"What do you mean? Isn't it better to have more people, so each of them has to run a shorter distance? Wouldn't that be easier?"

"It's certainly true that if fifteen people had to split the burden equally, each person would have less to do. But the larger the group, the higher the probability that you'll have slow students on your team. I can count the number of people who are good at running long-distance marathons on my fingers."

"Yeah, you've got a point."

"In other words, this is our chance to close the gap."

"But that's assumin' our entire group's athletic, right?"

Ishizaki looked around. I could be classified as athletic, but since we couldn't really count upon Kouenji, that meant the only other runner in the group was Hashimoto. We didn't exactly have a surplus of speedy people.

"This is going to sound pathetic, but...despite saying all that, I probably won't be of any use," said Keisei.

He knew his limitations best. Of everyone in the group, Keisei had the worst stamina and speed. But as the representative, he came up with a plan.

"The long-distance relay is eighteen kilometers. The rules state that every person has to run a minimum of 1.2 kilometers. So in a group of fifteen, everyone would have to run the same distance: 1.2 kilometers each. However, in a group of ten people, you can make significant changes to how you allocate the distances."

"We can't just say someone's injured and can't participate, can we?"

"Any absence on that day due to injury or illness will result in a penalty. Not only will that cause more trouble for the remaining people, it also costs us time. That's no good. Plus, the changeover point has to be every 1.2 kilometers."

The school was working hard to squash any loopholes. Students would have to do what was required of them. So Keisei and Yahiko, who lacked confidence in their speed, would have to run the minimum distance of 1.2 kilometers. The three guys from Class B might be placed at that bare minimum too.

Albert was reasonably fast, but the problem was his stamina. Even if everyone else in the group ran the bare minimum distance, the remaining four people would each have to run an average of 2.7 kilometers, if not more... but students who were skilled in long-distance marathon running might very well be capable of that. Which meant the thoughts crossing my mind were exactly what Keisei was getting at.

"In that case, I'll run 3...nah, I'll do 3.6 kilometers," declared Ishizaki. He was certainly one of the few members in our group who could handle it.

Another person raised his hand.

"In that case, it looks like I gotta do the same thing. I'm not too shabby when it comes to running long distances myself," said Hashimoto. Two of the most qualified members of the group had earnestly promised to shoulder a significant burden. That meant we'd covered 7.2 kilometers.

"Thank you."

Keisei bowed in gratitude. If this was how things were going, I supposed I needed to cover a certain amount myself.

"Then...I'll try to do what I can. I don't know how fast I can run it, though," I told Keisei.

"Is that okay, Kiyotaka?"

"Just don't expect too much from me."

However, the crucial part was what came next. The man known as Kouenji—the person with the highest potential here, the person who topped our class in stamina and athleticism, whom not even Sudou would hold a candle to. The more Kouenji ran, the easier it would be for the other students. He would probably run the minimum distance of 1.2 kilometers, but he had yet to promise to do anything more than that.

More importantly, there was no telling if he would *seriously* run. Even if the nine of us ran our hearts out, we'd be done for if Kouenji decided to stroll along.

"Kouenji. I would like you to run too." It was precisely because Keisei was aware of being the weakest link himself that he bowed his head even lower when addressing Kouenji.

Kouenji sat in bed, looking at his own fingernails and smiling.

"Kouenji."

Keisei calmly called his name once more.

"I will run, of course. However, unlike those fellows, I am not so inclined to run long distances," said Kouenji.

Well, it wouldn't have been like him to agree right off the bat. Ishizaki glared at Kouenji but didn't attempt to hound him. The last few days had made him begin to understand Kouenji's actions better, including their apparent meaninglessness.

"I would like to avoid our group placing last."

"I suppose so. I understand what you're saying, Glasses-kun."

Shifting his gaze away from his fingernails, Kouenji glanced at Keisei.

"Even if running long-distance is impossible, I will at least run 1.2 kilometers with serious effort."

Everyone in the group looked at Kouenji.

"I cannot make any promises. Even if our group does place last, it's not as though I will be expelled. Only you, the representative, will be. You surely wouldn't do something so *inhuman* as drag a classmate to ruin with you. Isn't that right?"

If the representative had been someone like Ishizaki

or Yahiko, then perhaps Kouenji would have run. But since it was Keisei, a classmate, he figured he was safe. If we threatened him with expulsion regardless, there was a slight chance we might be able to get him to run here and now—but only at the cost of never having his cooperation ever again.

"Then tell me. What do we have to do to get you to cooperate? If paying you private points will help, I'll do that," said Keisei. Again, it was precisely because he understood he was the greatest liability in that group that he was willing to pay out of his own pocket.

"Don't carry that burden alone, Yukimura," Hashimoto said. "I don't have much, but I've got points."

"I'll pay too."

Yahiko and the other guys joined in, agreeing to help out. I guess it was like they said, every little bit counts. If the nine of us pooled our points, we'd end up with a fairly large sum. How would Kouenji react to the unified wishes of the entire group?

"Unfortunately for you, I'm not exactly struggling as far as private points are concerned. Besides, I could lead a fulfilling life at school even if I didn't have any points, you see."

As I'd anticipated, he wasn't even slightly moved by our promise of cash. Asking him to do his best for the group's sake was clearly pointless, too. Everyone in the group, myself included, had racked their brains for the last few days, trying to figure out how to get Kouenji to cooperate. Our seniors had tried too. And every attempt had ended in failure.

"Are you saying that you won't run for us?"

"Yes, I suppose so," said Kouenji after a moment's thought. "It doesn't seem that I will be an asset to you all," he added.

Ishizaki, who'd held himself back so far, stood up to go for Kouenji, but Keisei stopped him.

"However, rest assured about one thing. While I don't intend to do anything more than what is required, I will do the bare minimum. I have my own way of doing things, you see."

"So that means...you'll produce average results?"

"That is correct. Of course, even by doing the bare minimum, I will still most likely produce superior results. I suppose this is good news for you all, isn't it?"

I had a feeling that everyone present understood what he meant when he said that. We'd started to feel like a team at long last, even if it was just barely so. We'd started thinking about what we could do for each other, as friends.

My analysis of the situation told me that the reality, however, was that Kouenji was acting from purely selfish motives. He'd behaved in completely unprecedented ways in every exam we'd had so far, but none of those things he did were enough to get him expelled. Kouenji had figured that there was a 99 percent chance that Keisei wouldn't drag him down with him, but that still left the possibility, no matter how slim, of it happening. If he did perform poorly, the school would make note of it, and then he'd have no way of escaping the solidarity rule if it was invoked against him. A guy like him wouldn't make that mistake.

"Whaddya mean, excellent results? You can't even do something like *zazen* right."

"Heh. I mastered things like *zazen* in my early childhood. It's *no problem*."

"What was your childhood like?" someone asked.

Kouenji just laughed, ignoring the question. Still, this might be good enough for Keisei. Even though Kouenji had no intention of cooperating with us, he promised to do the bare minimum. That alone was huge. As his classmates, we knew the sheer extent of his potential.

There were still several unknowns, like *zazen* and the written test, but we could at least place our faith in Kouenji's physical fitness for the marathon.

• •

WITH ONE PROBLEM SOLVED, it was time for our morning dusting. When Keisei was about to start cleaning, Ishizaki went over and picked up the dustcloth.

"Take a break. If you can't run in the relay, that'll be worse."

"Well, but—"

"Rest. In exchange, do your best on the written exam. Get at least 120 percent, will ya?"

"Okay. It's impossible to get 120 percent, but I'll shoot for 100..."

It seemed Ishizaki finally understood what it meant to give and take. Keisei thanked him gratefully and sat down.

"Quite prudent of you, Delinquent-kun."

"Shut your piehole or I'll kill ya, Kouenji. You haven't done a single damn thing since the first damn day!"

"Is that so? Ha ha ha!"

Kouenji didn't take a dustcloth or broom. Instead, he left, strolling outside to be in nature. Even with the second- and third-years watching, he acted brash.

"That dude is a disease. Can you guys even make it to the upper classes with him along for the ride?"

Even the Class D folks felt sorry for us.

"...I can't say I'm confident."

Keisei had always felt strongly about climbing the ranks, but Kouenji was a most bizarre variable. His performance tomorrow would have a huge impact on our scores. He'd promised to do the bare minimum during our morning discussion, but that guaranteed nothing. It was entirely possible he'd skip out on his duties as soon as he was out of sight.

If he refused to even participate in something like cleaning, there was a very real chance that we might come in last place. If that happened, even the upperclassmen who'd turned a blind eye to him so far might suddenly bare their fangs at him. While I generally thought of Kouenji as a calculating person who wouldn't do something so foolish, his complete and total irrationality made me wary of the possibility that he might betray my expectations.

Sensing Keisei's anxiety, Ishizaki approached.

"Don't worry. We just gotta compensate for him."

"That sure doesn't sound like you. You've become much more understanding in only a day."

"Shut it, Hashimoto. What, you got a problem?!"

"No problem. Our group's ranking impacts my own plans. I'd like for us to score at least one spot above the lowest rank. Isn't that right, Yahiko?"

"Well, yeah. Since our group's a handful, we have no choice but to do our best. If we get a poor score, Katsuragi-san will be disappointed in us," said Yahiko.

Hashimoto had a wry smile on his face as he smacked Yahiko, who was focused on Katsuragi as always, lightly on the shoulder. Yahiko had to be aware he'd hold us back during activities like the marathon. He'd been behaving pretty humbly since the test started.

"I've squared off against Katsuragi many times on Sakayanagi's orders. You probably resent me for that, but right now we're allies for real. Please forget about the past."

"Hmm. Maybe."

Yahiko didn't shout or make a scene, but I got the sense his trust in Hashimoto had its limits. Some part of him likely couldn't forgive Hashimoto for the way Katsuragi had been hindered by his own classmates so far.

"Didn't you set up Katsuragi-san to be the representative?" asked Yahiko.

"I had nothing to do with that. That was Matoba's plan."

Yahiko didn't seem convinced. But he controlled himself, choosing not to disrupt the group. I had to give him credit for that.

7.2

● ●

I T WAS OUR FINAL DINNER before the exam. I spotted Ichinose walking past, carrying a tray, and called out to her. I wasn't attempting to draw information out of her. It was just that, well...something seemed a little off about her.

"Is something bothering you?"

"Huh? Oh, Ayanokouji-kun. Nothing, really. I was just thinking about this and that."

"You're facing a difficult problem, huh?"

Ichinose seemed about to walk away but then stopped. "The final test is tomorrow. What do you think about this exam, Ayanokouji-kun?"

"That's a really roundabout question."

"I want you to tell me your honest thoughts."

"I guess it seems different from the exams we've

had until now. A little tougher. There's a high risk of expulsion."

"I see. But we're in our third semester now. Isn't it only natural that things would get more difficult?"

"I guess."

"Speaking of risks, this whole representative system is scary, huh? Becoming the leader of a group."

"Yeah."

"Being the representative is very risky, but...becoming the representative for the sake of winning is also important, right?"

I didn't argue, just listened intently to what she had to say.

"Even if you say there's the risk of expulsion, I guess it's kind of like...that's all up in the air somehow. Like it doesn't really feel real. ...To be honest, there's a great deal that's still hidden from me. But what I'm really scared of isn't losing class points or private points."

"You're talking about your classmates?"

"Yeah. The risk of losing one of them is unfathomable."

"If a classmate were expelled, what would you intend to do?" I asked.

"What would I do?" Ichinose slowly looked up, a thin smile on her face. "Ayanokouji-kun, you really are a smart guy, aren't you?"

"Why do you say that?"

"I mean, normally, there's nothing you can do if someone's expelled, right? But you know there's always a way."

"It was a hypothetical question."

"If it were really a hypothetical, you wouldn't have used the word *intend*, would you? You'd say, 'What would happen?' or phrase it completely differently, like, 'Would your class be okay?' or something."

"Sorry. You're giving me way too much credit. My language skills aren't that advanced."

"Still. I think you have a very respectable sense of intuition."

She then told me she'd gotten too caught up in chatting and that she'd see me later. Ichinose walked off, probably burdened with plenty of things she needed to ponder alone. I watched other students call out to her as she went. Being popular was rough. Even when you just wanted some time to think, people wouldn't leave you alone.

Still, Ichinose always had a smile on her face. But that didn't seem to be the case today.

"Yeah. Sorry, I'm just not feeling up to it today," said Ichinose, walking away from two girls whom she was close to. She sounded dispirited. "Sorry. I just have some things going on. I feel like I'd like to be alone for today."

This was no act. She seemed like a completely different person from when our first day at this camp.

Seeing that, I understood. Sakayanagi had made her move. The coming storm wasn't just going to hit the guys. The girls might just be in for it, too.

7.3

INCE IT WAS THE FINAL DAY before the exam, things had changed dramatically. The mood in the cafeteria remained unchanged, but you could clearly tell who was laughing and who was depressed. In short, there was a clear distinction between those whose groups were doing well and those whose groups were not.

As I stepped out into the hallway, Kei was there, leaning against the wall near the entrance to the cafeteria.

She casually slipped me a piece of paper as I passed by, then immediately entered the cafeteria, probably going to meet up with her friends. As we parted ways, I looked at the slip of paper, then shredded it and divided the pieces up between several trash bins placed all around the building.

She'd held on pretty well throughout the week, but it seemed she was finally at her limit.

I walked to a corner of the school building, where the

person whom Kei had been keeping an eye on for me was trying to grab some alone time. Solitude was a limited resource at this camp. There was the middle of the night, sure, but others would notice if you were gone from your shared room for a long period of time. Your best option was to make use of the time when everyone was gathered in the cafeteria.

As I followed the person in question, she crouched down, like she was trying to hide. She didn't notice me there. I watched her trying to hold back tears, and I hesitated, wondering what to do.

But no matter how hard it might be for someone to find this place, there was no telling when another student might just show up. I should wrap this up fast.

"If you're in some kind of trouble...maybe you should talk to the former student council president?"

"Huh?!"

Third-year Class A student Tachibana Akane looked up at me. Panicked at being seen in such a pathetic state, she quickly wiped her tears away.

"Wh-what is it?"

"Nothing. Just exactly what I said."

"I'm not in any trouble or anything."

"If you're crying even though you're not in trouble, that might be a problem in and of itself."

"I'm not crying!"

As she said that, Tachibana averted her eyes from me. She probably wasn't moving from the spot she was in because she knew her reddened eyes and the wetness on her face would be clearly visible if she went somewhere brightly lit.

"Sometimes I just want to be alone."

"True. We don't get much private time, huh?"

Bathroom breaks were it, more or less, and you could only use those for so long. There were always students coming and going, seeing you there.

"For the record, I'm on Former President Horikita's side."

That was a lie. But if I said that, Tachibana would trust me more.

"Doesn't matter. You're not going to be any help."

Well...when she put it like that, I had no response. In fact, I might accidentally give away something I didn't want to if I kept going.

"Just consider the fact that it's better if we're not enemies."

"Okay, can you stop talking to your seniors in such a casual way? I haven't said anything about it to you until now because Horikita-kun was there, but..."

Rather than the rebuke, what piqued my curiosity was the fact that she called him "Horikita-kun." She usually continued to refer to him as President Horikita, which was odd in its own right, given he was no longer in office. She could tack on the word *former* before that title, but the way Tachibana referred to him was strange.

"You... It must be nice being a first-year. So carefree."

"Wow, you sound pretty scared. Are you anxious about the test tomorrow?"

"I don't feel anything. The representative's at stake and all, but things aren't bad between people in our group or anything. If anything, things are going great."

"In that case, why are you crying?"

"I-I told you, I wasn't crying!"

When I pointed at Tachibana's eyes, she panicked and touched her face to check for any fresh tears that might have welled up. When she realized I'd fooled her, she glared at me.

"Horikita-kun...is the one that I'm worried about," she said.

That was a lie...and at the same time not. But I wouldn't touch that just yet.

"Worry, huh? Is there really anything to worry about when it comes to that guy?"

"Horikita-kun... Horikita-kun has been fighting alone for a long time. He's been fighting the second- and third-years all this time. You can't possibly understand how difficult it is to have to face everyone all by yourself."

True. I'd never understand that, even if I tried.

"I know a little bit about how the second-years, particularly Nagumo, are his enemies," I said. "But he has enemies among the third-years too? Not many people would want to rebel against the former student council president, right?"

"Do you take Horikita-kun for some kind of dictator? Even when he was student council president, he never did just as he pleased, like Nagumo-kun. You can never afford to let your guard down in any test."

I had never gotten the opportunity to learn about the third-years' internal affairs. I didn't know a single thing about the elder Horikita's background. But if she said they couldn't afford to let their guard down in any exam, that meant...

"Wait. You mean the class conflict among the third-years is still ongoing?"

"If Horikita-kun fails, then Class A will definitely fall."

"Huh."

Nagumo had said the same thing. He'd mentioned the gap between third-year Classes A and B was only 312 points. If Horikita's brother was the main weapon at Class A's disposal, or if Class B had a remarkably skilled student up their sleeve, it was certainly possible their lead might be overturned.

"So even he's just a normal student."

"Horikita-kun is...! Nothing. Forget it."

She raised her voice unintentionally but then quieted herself. Tachibana began to speak, slower this time, as though letting her frustration spill forth.

"It's because the rest of us in Class A are always holding the class back. We lost a ton of class points that we shouldn't have, and even private points, too... He's always sacrificing himself to protect his comrades."

If what Tachibana was saying was true, then Horikita's brother was much like Hirata—which surprised me, to be honest. Of course, if Tachibana, who was actually *in* the third-year Class A, said it...there had to be some degree of truth to it. If I had to guess, there had probably been a lot of occasions when the elder Horikita handled things behind the scenes, so no one saw what a virtuous person he was. And the person who'd seen him do those things, by his side more often than anyone else, was this girl here.

"So you're depressed by the current situation?"

"Even I've heard about what's going on with the boys. Including the fact that Nagumo-kun challenged Horikita-kun to a contest, and because of that, he can't make a move. We can't help him at all."

"That depends on how tenacious you are, doesn't it?"

"I know that."

Fresh tears may have welled up in her eyes, because Tachibana wiped them with her arm once more. Her concern for Horikita's brother may have been one reason for her tears, but I was betting there was more to it.

"You're in some kind of trouble, aren't you?"

"I'm not. Not really."

"Not really?"

"You're persistent, aren't you? I'm not in any kind of trouble."

"If you say so, I must be mistaken."

"You are. Please don't say anything weird to Horikita-kun."

"Okay."

With that stern warning, Tachibana headed back to the cafeteria. She probably didn't want Horikita's brother to learn the truth of whatever was going on with her. But she'd made an error in judgment. This wasn't a problem you could solve by sacrificing yourself.

"I suppose this means it's checkmate if I don't make a move, huh?"

Watching Tachibana's frail, slender back as she walked off, I was sure of that fact.

7.4

IT WAS MIDNIGHT when I was woken up by a slight creaking sound. A lone student was moving in the pitch darkness. Of course, despite the lack of visibility, I still knew who it was—Hashimoto, who was supposed to be sleeping in the bunk above me right now. He descended from the top bunk without making a sound and left the room without even bringing a flashlight with him. When he was gone, I slowly sat up.

It was most likely a bathroom break, but there were other possibilities too. What caught my attention was the fact that, over the course of the last week, Hashimoto hadn't once slipped out of the room in the middle of the night to go to the bathroom.

After giving him a slight head start, I got up and followed. On the off chance that he happened to be standing outside the door, I'd just say I'd gotten up to use the bathroom too. We shared the same bunk bed; Hashimoto would just think he'd woken me up.

I stealthily went into the corridor. Even though the only illumination came from the emergency lighting and a sliver of moonlight, I could walk without a flashlight. Hashimoto headed toward the bathroom, then disappeared from view. I started following him. I quickly saw him turn left, even though the bathroom was straight down the hall.

So he didn't need the bathroom, apparently. Hashimoto descended to the first floor and went outside, still wearing his indoor slippers. I hid myself, hugging the wall. There were no other students around. Maybe he simply came outside to get some fresh air because he couldn't sleep. Or perhaps he was waiting for someone?

I learned the answer to my question right away.

Sensing that he was going to turn my way, I moved to a different spot when I saw another shadow, which I assumed was his target. The shadow moved along the same path as Hashimoto and went outside. It was so quiet you couldn't even hear insects, which meant even a whisper sounded clear as a bell.

"Hey, Ryuuen," Hashimoto said.

"The hell do you want with me?"

"I just wanted to chat. I mean, you stand out way too much in the cafeteria, dude. The only time I can talk to you is the middle of the night."

"On the last day?"

"Yeah. I called you here *because* it's the last day. Right now, everyone else is sound asleep."

"I see. Guess you got a point."

No students would deliberately stay up late into the night when there was an exam the next day. Still, Ryuuen and Hashimoto...that was a pairing I wouldn't have expected. Then again, Ryuuen had formed a relationship with Class A back during our time on the uninhabited island. I wouldn't be surprised if Hashimoto had played the part of intermediary.

"Look, I'm not good at talking about stuff in a roundabout way. So I want to hear a straight answer. Did you really quit being the class leader?"

"Hee hee hee. Doesn't seem like you believe it, huh?"

"At the very least, I don't buy that Ishizaki and the others worked you over," replied Hashimoto, zeroing in on the detail that stuck out to him. True, the idea of Ishizaki beating Ryuuen was pretty dumb.

"Ishizaki aside, Albert's trouble. If we really went head-to-head with one another, it'd be brutal."

"I see. Well, Albert's certainly a threat, I guess. But the

Ryuuen Kakeru I know isn't the kind of guy to cower before an opponent. If anything, he's the sort of guy who's
always thinking up counterattacks, isn't he?"

Rather than diminish Hashimoto's suspicions, what
Ryuuen had said only heightened them.

"I just got tired of trying to unite people who keep
rebelling against me. As long as I continue to bleed you
Class A folks dry, I'm in the clear. I ain't got any obliga-
tion to those other guys."

"I see. So that's it."

"Did I convince you?"

"Not sure. I'm still fifty-fifty. Personally, I think I want
you to fight back against the situation you're in."

"So you can score some more pocket change?"

"Yep. I want the 'promise of Class A.' Just like you."

If you could save up twenty million points, then you
could buy the right to move into A Class. A student
with the means to do that could rest easy—an enviable
situation. Making that goal a reality was difficult, but it
seemed Hashimoto was one of the students aiming to do
just that.

"If the promise of victory is what you crave, I'm guessing you're prepared to dispose of Sakayanagi?"

"If necessary."

Hashimoto continued.

"Selling out Sakayanagi doesn't come cheap, Ryuuen. Right now, she's at the top of our class. I'm on the winning team. Get it?"

"We'll see how much of an opportunist you really are."

"I'm pretty good at making my way in the world. You should know that I can come out on top pretty well. Anyway, I'm glad I could talk with you directly. Doesn't look like you've lost your fire."

Hashimoto yawned, then added one last thing.

"When you got overtaken by Hirata's class, I wondered what the hell you were even doing. But they might be a tough bunch after all."

"Huh?"

"If you examine each member with a level head, you can see they're pretty evenly matched. I'd like for them to be crushed as soon as possible."

"Huh. To think a guy like you would be sizing them up. Any particular guy caught your interest?"

"Kouenji is a threat, at the very least. To be honest, if he started acting to his class's advantage, there's no telling what would happen to Class A. They also have academically gifted students like Hirata and Yukimura, and Sudou, who's easily one of the most athletic students in our grade."

"I don't know about those other guys, but I can't imagine Sudou will do anything terribly special."

Hashimoto chuckled in agreement.

"Anyway, there's no telling what will happen, but here's something to keep in mind. Even if Hirata's group does manage to make it all the way to Class A, I'm fine as long as there's room for me to slip in there too."

"I doubt you have that much power. Try not to get burned," said Ryuuen mockingly, as if to end the conversation there.

"It's shitty, but dragging this out is just a hassle."

"Yeah."

I thought they'd wrap up there, so I prepared to move. Hashimoto would probably head back to the room. If I wasn't asleep before he got back, he might suspect something.

But I sensed someone else approaching and stopped in my tracks. One of the two people who drew near immediately noticed Ryuuen and Hashimoto and called out to them.

"What's up, first-years? Having a secret meeting at a time like this, huh?"

"Huh?"

Nagumo Miyabi and Horikita Manabu stood before the two conspirators. Ryuuen paused for a moment, then immediately seemed to lose interest and made to leave. He walked right toward Nagumo, who didn't budge.

"Outta the way."

Nagumo laughed, like he found Ryuuen's glare amusing. Meanwhile Hashimoto, who had come back into the corridor to see what was going on, locked eyes with Nagumo.

"I've heard you're quite the delinquent. Your name's Ryuuen, right? I'm going to have a little chat with Horikita-senpai, but you should come along." Nagumo beckoned Hashimoto, summoning him to join them too.

"Ain't interested," said Ryuuen, shoulder-checking Nagumo as he passed.

"Wow, you're confident. Not scared of me, Ryuuen?"

"Doesn't matter if you're student council president or whatever. I'll crush anyone who gets in my way."

"Heh."

Nagumo seemed to have a certain degree of interest in Ryuuen, who wasn't bothered a bit.

"I don't dislike people like you. But you're not really fit to be part of my student council."

As Ryuuen tried to walk away, Nagumo called out to him once again.

"Hey, how about you join this wager, as a third party? Which group do you think will place higher in today's special exam, mine, or Horikita-senpai's? How about ten thousand points a head? No matter which side you bet on, I'll pay up if you're right on the money. If you're wrong, though, you gotta pay up."

"That's dumb. Not interested in that kind of money."

"Ten thousand is 'that kind of money', huh? You're in Class D, meaning you're always short on cash, right? Can't hurt to earn a little more."

"In that case, make it a million. I'll play along if you're willing to pay up," said Ryuuen, turning around.

"Hahaha! You're a funny guy, Ryuuen. Talk about a ballsy joke. You can go now."

Apparently, he thought Ryuuen's proposal was a joke.

"If you don't got the guts to pay up that much, don't bother asking me to make a bet."

"Hey, you. First-year. You think Ryuuen can pay that much?" Nagumo asked Hashimoto.

Since Hashimoto was aware of Ryuuen's secret arrangement with Class A, he knew Ryuuen definitely had enough. But...

"Not sure. We're in different classes, so I can't really say."

"If we had our phones, we could check. I wouldn't mind playing along then. Too bad."

Looked like the wager wasn't going to happen then. Hashimoto moved to make his escape, and Nagumo shifted his gaze over to Horikita.

"Horikita-senpai. Please abstain from taking the exam tomorrow," Nagumo said abruptly. Ryuuen continued walking, seemingly uninterested, but Hashimoto stopped in his tracks.

"Abstain?"

"That's right."

"That's an even worse joke than Ryuuen's."

"Actually, I'm being quite serious." Nagumo added something else. "It's for your own sake, senpai."

"Please explain it to me in a way I can understand. You have a habit of just saying everything in your head, and it seems like you have yet to address that."

"Sorry. Being able to see too far into the future is a curse. Anyway, if you don't kindly abstain tomorrow, senpai, you'll regret it. What I'm saying is that I'm trying to help you. I could just put the hurt on you without warning, but that would just be heartless, wouldn't it?"

"What are you planning? Depending on what it is, I may not accept."

"I understand. The rules of our contest are that we have to fight fair and square, without involving any third parties. But the way things are, if the exam takes place, we won't know which of us will win until we get a look at the results. Of course, it's only to be expected that this will be a close race. But that's exactly why I want to win. And I've been taking steps to ensure I do."

"Is that why you want me to abstain?"

"Yes. Because abstaining will allow you to get through this with the least amount of damage, senpai. Are you aware of the strategic groundwork that I've laid? No, you aren't, are you? There isn't a single student at this school who can read my thoughts. That's what this is. Even your little favorite is the same... Who was that first-year again?"

Nagumo looked intentionally at Hashimoto. But there was no way Hashimoto knew.

"Ah, that's right. If I recall, he's in the same group as that first-year. Ayanokouji Kiyotaka." Nagumo clearly emphasized my name, as though he were trying to make Hashimoto aware of it. "What do you think, Hashimoto? About Ayanokouji."

"What do I...? Well, I think he's just a normal student."

Hashimoto was visibly shaken after unexpectedly hearing my name come up.

"I know, right? But Horikita-senpai here seems to value Ayanokouji over all other first-years."

"Maybe because he performed well at the relay during the Sports Festival?"

"Well, that would make sense. But that doesn't seem to be all there is to it. See, Horikita-senpai prizes Ayanokouji above even Sakayanagi, even Ryuuen, even Ichinose. Since you're in the same group as him, I thought you might have noticed something."

"No."

"Why is that, senpai? Please, I think it's about time you tell me the reason."

"You're reaching, Nagumo. When have I spoken highly of Ayanokouji? There is nothing to be gained by spreading lies. Stop teasing the first-years."

"Sorry, senpai. I suppose you're right. My bad, Hashimoto. That was a little joke."

"Is that so...?"

I didn't like where this conversation was headed, but it was time I got out of there. The three of them were blocking the corridor, so I needed to use the stairs on the opposite end of the building. It meant taking a detour, but I decided to go the alternate route. I had to be back by the time Hashimoto returned, or it might end up making him suspect there was something to what Nagumo was saying.

A few minutes after I returned, Hashimoto quietly entered the room. I felt his gaze fall upon me from the top bunk, but only for a moment. Afterward, he went to sleep.

8

THE SECOND HALF OF
THE GIRLS' BATTLE:
HORIKITA SUZUNE

T HE FINAL TEST would be the next day. The rest of the
student body was busy gobbling down their dinner when
I, Horikita Suzune, made contact with a certain someone
inside our room. With everyone else in the cafeteria at the
time, it was simple for the two of us to make contact.

"Look, Horikita-san. To be honest with you, I don't
think you're seeing the current situation for what it is."

Standing before me was Kushida-san, a serious look
in her eyes. In the cramped confines of the camp school,
with eyes and ears everywhere, I couldn't neglect to keep
tabs on her—even though it was her public-facing per-
sona that stood before me now.

"I'm not seeing the current situation? What do you
mean by that?"

"You forced me to be in the same group as you, for the purpose of keeping me under surveillance...or to have me acknowledge you as a comrade. Is that right?"

She spoke in her normal, friendly tone of voice, clearly operating on the assumption that someone might enter the room at any moment. But there was something more forceful than usual to the way she said it, almost certainly because she felt secure that I couldn't pull any tricks like recording our conversation with my smartphone in our current situation. Personally, I welcomed her honesty. If she always kept her true nature hidden, we'd never move forward.

"I won't deny that those objectives are part of it," I said.

I made sure to emphasize *part* quite strongly, but Kushida-san ignored it.

"You seem to be acting on your personal feelings. I wonder how that will work as a strategy. It's certainly true that you and I don't get along, Horikita-san. But if you were thinking about the group's scores...no, if you were thinking about your *class*, shouldn't you keep your personal feelings out of it?" said Kushida-san, crossing her arms with a sigh, as if thrusting her honest opinion at me. "You've made me, and me alone, your priority. Winning and losing are just secondary concerns. Am I wrong?"

"I can't deny that either."

"So you admit it."

Frankly, there was no way I could deny it. Ever since the Paper Shuffle, I'd considered Kushida-san my primary concern. I even invited her out for tea during winter vacation. I was doing things I'd never done before.

"It doesn't matter what you do," she said. "Enough already. I want you to understand that."

"Unfortunately, I'm afraid I can't let this go."

So long as my problems with Kushida-san went unresolved, I couldn't move forward.

"Look, it's not my place to say this, but have you forgotten about how you dragged me out in front of the student council president and made me swear I wouldn't do anything? Putting aside my own feelings, which I *will not get over,* I promised I wouldn't do anything to sabotage you, Horikita-san. I thought you'd at least trust me that much. Or did you think I'd break my promise right away?"

I couldn't answer her question with words. Kushida-san probably understood my feelings. What she said was half correct; even though I expected she'd keep her promise, however reluctantly, I also thought she might be working behind the scenes to get me expelled. Those two instincts clashed within me.

If I truly trusted Kushida-san, I wouldn't feel the need to stick by her all hours of the day. Moreover, while my brother isn't the sort who would say anything to anyone else, once he graduated, the oath she swore would be meaningless. If I were to take action, it would have to be soon. Time was of the essence.

"I want you to trust me," I told her, deciding to get straight to the point.

"Wow, you're blunt."

Despite apparently taking what I said at face value, Kushida-san wore a thin smile on her face. But it wasn't a smile of agreement. I couldn't let myself be mistaken on that count.

"No matter what, I will not say anything to anyone about your past. What do I have to do to make you believe me?"

"Unfortunately, there's no way you can convince me," replied Kushida-san flatly.

"I gain nothing by telling people."

"You're certainly right about that. If I *did* find out you told someone, I'd show no mercy. I might even destroy the entire class, just like I did back in junior high. As someone who's aiming for Class A, you obviously wouldn't put yourself in jeopardy. At least, that's what you'd assume," said Kushida-san.

She seemed to understand. So what was the problem?

"But if you ask me, our current environment's a little *cramped*."

"Cramped?"

"For example, would you obey a stranger who puts a knife to the back of your neck and says he'll hurt you if you don't cooperate? There's a difference between a situation where you can't be hurt even if someone tried to and a situation where someone *could* hurt you if they wanted to. You understand, don't you?"

Kushida-san didn't trust anyone. She didn't make her decisions based on whether they advantaged or disadvantaged her; she simply couldn't stand anyone else holding power over her. That's why she wanted to eliminate me. The problem was I couldn't let go of the knife, even if I wanted to.

"Aren't you just strangling yourself with your own two hands then?" I said. "As a matter of fact, the number of people who know about you are slowly but surely increasing."

"That's right. I will admit that the situation has gotten more dire."

"You're clever. You're above average in both academics and athletics, and you have the best communication skills in our grade level... No, depending on how you look at it, you might even be able to say you're the best in the school. Even talking to you now, I'm impressed by your quick thinking. You could be an incredible asset to our class if you simply cooperated with us. You'd be even more beloved by your peers too."

"Do you honestly not get that your know-it-all tone irritates me more than anything else? You're talking this way because you know my true personality. I can't stand that. If you didn't know anything about me, you wouldn't be saying these things."

"That's..."

She would never accept anyone knowing about her past. Her resolve was clear.

"You're smarter than me. Wouldn't you do just fine even at another school? Besides, you came here so you could be at the same school as your older brother. Right, Horikita-san? But your brother will be graduating soon, so you won't need to force yourself to stay. You could study at a different school, go on to college or land a job. Wouldn't that be fine?" asked Kushida-san.

She was trying to cut our conversation short, as though saying that trying to talk to her any longer would just be a waste of time. I let out a quiet sigh.

"I'll be quiet for now. But I will never trust or cooperate with you, Horikita-san. Until either you or I are gone from this school, we'll never be okay. No matter how many times we have this conversation. You'd do well to remember that."

"I understand. I'll leave things for today."

"Not just today. This is the last time."

Kushida-san walked out of the room, leaving me with those parting words.

"I really am powerless, aren't I?"

I had very few comrades I could trust. Ayanokouji-kun seemed like the one I could most often rely on, but he and I had grown more distant of late, probably because I forced him to talk about the student council in front of Kushida-san. But I couldn't back down. I had to keep her close to protect myself.

Even if it cost me his cooperation, I would choose Kushida-san. No—I *must* choose her.

9 BLIND SPOT

IT WAS THE FINAL DAY of camp, the day when our groups would be ranked according to the special exam. During this last week, the twenty-six or so small groups had passed time in their own unique ways. Some groups had gotten to know one another better and worked well together. Others were on the verge of collapse. Others had completed their daily tasks with indifference, growing neither closer nor further apart.

At first, our group had been a disaster. However, we'd grown significantly closer to one another by the end. I mean, we weren't perfect. At best, we were a ragtag lot. This was a temporary alliance—come tomorrow, we'd be enemies again. There was a certain sense of sadness at the thought of our group activities coming to an end.

"For the time being, we've done all we can. No matter what the outcome, we have no regrets."

"I think so too. Thanks for being our representative, Yukimura."

Ishizaki and Yukimura shook hands.

"No matter what happens, let's give it our all."

"Let's do it."

The other guys complimented each other and shook on it. Afterward, we headed to our assigned classroom. There was nothing to worry about as far as group unity. Our biggest concern was Kouenji.

Right now, he seemed calm, quietly following us. But no one could predict when he might suddenly cut loose. The second- and third-years from our large group had already arrived, so we hurried to our seats in a bit of a panic just as the chime sounded. The teacher entered and began to explain the contents of the exam.

Even though we'd gathered in our large group, the exam would be administered to the small groups by grade level. The large groups would affect the overall ranking when the scores were tallied. No matter how vast the camp grounds, if everyone tried doing all the same activities at the same time, we'd be crammed in together.

The four sections of the exam were as expected. They included *Zen*, *Speech*, *Long-Distance Relay Race*, and

Written Exam. We first-year students would begin with *zazen*. Then we headed to the next classroom for our written exam. We'd follow that up with the long-distance relay race and, finally, we'd give our speeches.

The second-years had a higher hurdle to jump right out of the gate, since they were starting with the long-distance relay. The third-years, apparently, were beginning with speeches.

9.1

AFTER WE FINISHED BREAKFAST, we headed to the *zazen* dojo. We were exempted from cleaning this morning. The exam began as soon as all of the first-year guys had gathered.

"Without further ado, we will begin. There are two criteria in determining your scores: your manners and posture upon entering this dojo, and the presence or absence of any disorder during *zazen*. After you've finished, you will stand by in your assigned classrooms until you are given instructions for your next exam. Starting now, I will call out names. Students whose names have been called will line up and begin taking the test. Class A, Katsuragi Kouhei. Class D, Ishizaki Daichi—"

The instructor continued to read names aloud. After

Katsuragi came Ishizaki. That was an unexpected development. The crowd murmured its surprise.

"Hurry up, Ishizaki. Next, first-year Class B, Beppu Ryouta."

Confused, Ishizaki got in line, panicking slightly.

"Is this a different order then usual?"

Keisei mentally prepared while panicking himself. We hadn't expected this. We'd performed *zazen* several times over the past week, but always in our small groups. This time around, the school was assigning spots randomly.

That meant students outside our comfort zone would be close to our personal bubble. That might seem like a trivial difference, but on the day of the exam, when people were tense to begin with, it made everything that much harder. The school's goal to shake things up was working.

Keisei was flustered. Then a large hand rested on his shoulder—Albert, offering a gesture of consideration to calm him down. Getting the message, Keisei looked like he had regained a little bit of his composure.

"Sorry. If I'm like this during the very first exam, it'll affect our group's morale."

Rather than consider the pressure of being the representative as a negative, Keisei thought of it as a positive. When his name was finally called, he responded clearly and entered the dojo. I was called before Albert, the second to last. Several instructors inside the dojo stood around holding clipboards and pens.

On top of that, there was a strange number of cameras installed throughout the dojo, perhaps to add certainty to the scoring. I already had the basics of *zazen* down in my head, so I wasn't going to slip up. Since it was very likely the scoring system was set up in such a way where you'd start with one hundred and have points deducted based on performance, I calculated that I would definitely have a perfect score.

After all, there wasn't any need for me to hold back in performing *zazen*. A slight distance away from me, Kouenji was participating too. He made no mistakes—in fact, he had beautiful posture. His movements were flawless. He'd never once seemed to take practice seriously, but I guess this was what you'd expect from him, huh?

Since we kept our eyes closed during the assessment, I couldn't be sure about the finer details. But I was sure we'd done well.

9.2

AFTER WE FINISHED with *zazen*, everyone began to disperse in silence. We were still being graded until we actually left the dojo. Under the watchful gaze of the instructors, the students silently exited and headed toward their respective classrooms as instructed.

Once everyone in our group gathered, Keisei slumped in his chair.

"Ugh, my legs went numb during the test."

"Did you make it?" asked Ishizaki. His legs might have suffered a similar fate, because he rubbed at them as he asked Keisei that question.

"I think so. But I might've gotten a few points taken off."

"Well, no use worryin' about it. Nothing ya can do now. Right, Ayanokouji?" said Hashimoto.

"That's right. Next up is Keisei's forte: the written exam. Just focus on that," I told him.

Nagumo's words from last night were probably still in Hashimoto's head. But he wasn't going to confront me directly about them, because he had no idea what Horikita's brother considered special about me in the first place.

Two other small groups of first-years were in the room with us. One of them was the group that Ryuuen was in, which Akito was the representative for. I could tell that Ishizaki and Albert shifted their gazes over toward Ryuuen, but Ryuuen, rather than look back at us, took his seat, alone. He didn't talk to anyone. He was part of the group, but at the same time, he wasn't. He gave off an air of being completely and utterly isolated.

"Huh, that's pretty weird," muttered Hashimoto, standing next to me. It would be easy for me to ignore him, but I supposed I'd play along a bit.

"What is?"

"Ishizaki and Albert's eyes. I don't get the impression that they hate him. If anything, they look sorrowful. Like pets whose master has abandoned them."

"I don't get it. Didn't Ishizaki and Albert get fed up with Ryuuen?"

"That's what they say, but...maybe there's something more to Ryuuen stepping down. Don't you think so?"

Hashimoto almost certainly had no evidence linking me to Ryuuen. It was likely he was trying to steer the conversation in that direction because Nagumo had expressed an interest in Ryuuen.

"Dunno. I'm not really familiar with other classes' goings-on."

"I see. Sorry for asking you something weird."

After the ten-minute break ended, we moved on to the written exam, which proved to be nothing special. They tested what we had learned during our time at the camp. If you had a good grasp of the main topics we'd covered, you could almost certainly get a perfect score. If you were a student who struggled, you would get somewhere between fifty and seventy points.

What should I do?

While everyone else around me put their heads down and worked away, I tried to figure out how many points I should allow myself to lose. They probably weren't going to make individual scores public, but I didn't want to let the school see me get successive perfect scores. There were a lot of students who had been trying to feel me out as of late. Honestly, I would much rather hold back and not score too high.

I decided I would miss just one question that people would consider difficult. That would give me a solid 95 or so. After I finished penning down all my answers, I was tempted to look out the window. I didn't want the teachers to think I was cheating, though, so I shut my eyes and waited for the end.

After the test, the groups assembled and assessed our scores. It wasn't like calculating our scores ourselves was going to change the results, and yet, I couldn't really help but wonder whether I got that one question right or wrong. I guessed forcing yourself to think differently was effective, to a certain degree.

Everyone in our group was here except for Kouenji, who'd left the classroom as soon as the test was over. Ishizaki, as expected, hadn't understood most of the questions. My insurance was going to come in handy. Still, the written exam had been easy overall, meaning every group probably scored high.

Based on what I'd seen in the dojo, the written exam and *zazen* test might not have resulted in a significant point gap between groups. Everyone seemed to have performed *zazen* with a certain degree of precision. Both tests were about demonstrating what you'd learned, so if you could pull that off, there likely wouldn't be a huge variation in scores. Of all the sections of the exam, it was the long-distance relay race that was likely to have the biggest impact.

If final scores were awarded based on where you

placed in the relay, you might assume that the group who got first place would have earned a perfect score... but that was probably too simple, huh? I had a feeling they'd be taking our times into consideration too. In fact, you might even score well if you came in sixth place but made good time in the race.

When we left the classroom, I saw a number of vans parked outside. It seemed they'd be taking us to the spot where the batons would be handed out. When we got into the van, we received additional instructions from the teachers.

Every individual student must run a minimum distance of 1.2 kilometers.

Baton passes are only allowed every 1.2 kilometers.

If a student is unable to finish the race due to an accident, or if they fail to meet the minimum requirements, they will be disqualified.

After the teachers explained those three points, they dropped off Keisei, our first runner, and the van drove on. We'd decided our running order by the students who weren't confident in their speed. Keisei was first. Next were Sumida, Tokitou, and Moriyama from Class B. Yahiko was fifth.

We placed them like that because there were relative dips and rises in the terrain during the early stages of the race. Also, it put as little pressure as possible on them to worry about being overtaken by other runners. Those five would run the minimum distance each. Thus, we'd knock out a total of six kilometers.

Next up would be Hashimoto. He'd run at full speed for 3.6 kilometers, including the turnaround point. Then Albert would take the baton and run for 1.2 kilometers before passing it to Ishizaki, who'd run 3.6 kilometers. I would've been fine with placing after Albert, but Keisei believed the transition would be smoother if classmates were placed together.

Kouenji would only be running 1.2 kilometers. I was going to run 2.4 and pass the baton to him for the last leg. That was the conclusion that Keisei had reached in the end. Kouenji was put last to give him a little more motivation to finish. He'd get the credit for crossing the finish line, and relieve some of our anxieties about him not passing on the baton.

The downside was that if anyone cut corners, we wouldn't know who was running late. After Ishizaki got out of the van, there were three of us left: the instructor who was driving, Kouenji, and me. They could have dropped us off first, since they were going around the turning point anyway, but I supposed they intended to drop us off in the order we were running.

All that remained for me to do was wait at my spot 3.6 kilometers away from the finish line.

The van started moving back in the direction we came from.

"Ayanokouji Boy. Allow me to ask you something plainly. Should we take first place in this race, what do you think will happen? Overall, I mean."

"...There's no way that I'd know the answer to that, even if you ask. Besides, our overall results are determined by the average score of the large group. So it depends on how well the upperclassmen perform, right?"

No matter how hard we try, it'd be difficult to reach first place if they dropped the ball.

"So you won't even lie to reassure me that there's a possibility of getting first place, hmm?" he asked.

"You're not the kind of guy who'd be cheered up if I said something like that, are you?"

"Hmm, I have to wonder. How about you allow me to relieve you of 1.2 kilometers? If I run at full speed, there's an extremely high chance we'll defeat the other groups," Kouenji whispered into my ear, leaning in close.

"Okay, what the hell brought this about?" I asked.

"Just a whim. A whim that can help you. Not a bad offer, no?"

"You mean to tell me that you'll take responsibility for running 2.4 kilometers *and* for making us place well?"

"My, there's no need to speak so formally. It's just a whim, after all."

"I see. Sorry, I'm turning you down. I can't change Keisei's strategy on my own."

"Heh. I see. Well, that's unfortunate," said Kouenji, retaking his seat.

I didn't know what he was planning, but I had no intention of going out on a limb and trusting him. If he could decide to help on a whim, he could change his mind back on a whim too. Kouenji had only promised to run the minimum required distance. That meant he'd probably hold himself back if he ran anything beyond those 1.2 kilometers. The proof was in how he'd dodged the question I gave him about taking responsibility.

Besides, if I ended up causing us unnecessary trouble because of a decision I made, there'd be hell to pay.

"It seems you're cleverer than I thought. But also quite boring."

If that was how he saw me, I was grateful for it.

I got out of the van and waited for Ishizaki at the marker 3.6 kilometers from the finish line.

"Hey, Ayanokouji-kun."

Naturally, there were other guys waiting there, too. Hirata greeted me.

"Huh, you're not the anchor?" he asked.

"Nope. Kouenji is going last. What about you? Is Sudou your anchor?"

"Yeah. He's raring to go—wants to run a lot. But with fifteen people, that's not really going to work."

Sudou's rivalry with Kouenji would probably flare up during the final lap of the race.

"Personally, I wish we'd had more people," I said. "It would probably have made things a little easier."

"At any rate, let's both do our best. As long as we don't fall below the school's standards, no one will be expelled, after all."

"Yeah."

While we waited, everyone was free to chat or quietly concentrate. Since water stations were placed every 1.2 kilometers, it was also possible to get a drink...though you increased your chances of a stomachache if you guzzled down water before you ran. One student, totally oblivious to the peril, sucked down the contents of a plastic water bottle.

"Ah, I'm so nervous," he muttered before turning around and locking eyes with me. It was the Professor. Maybe he wanted someone to talk to, because he approached me. "So, you're in this spot too, Ayanokouji-kun."

"A-Ayanokouji-kun? In this spot...?"

I couldn't believe my ears. The Professor I knew would have said something like "Honorable Ayanokouji-dono, art thou currently placed upon this land?"

"Ah. Well, I quit talking like that. I was doing it to play a character, but after getting that warning during *zazen,* I thought I'd knock it off."

"I see."

I couldn't hide my shock at hearing the Professor speak so normally. It didn't suit him at all. It was like the thing that made him *him* had disappeared. He felt like a placeholder now, like Student X, or Y, or whatever.

We went on to have a completely ordinary conversation, but to be honest, I didn't remember any of it. Guess just changing the way you talked could make a huge difference.

At any rate, I wondered if Keisei had successfully passed the baton. No matter how long it took, finishing the race was crucial. Cold as it might sound, even if our large group did place dead last or fell below the school's standard line, no harm would come my way.

Of course, I did genuinely think it'd be better if no one got expelled.

As I wondered how many minutes had passed, I finally saw a student coming our way. However, it wasn't

Ishizaki. It was someone from the mostly Class B group led by Kanzaki. More students began to arrive, one after the other. After a close struggle with the runner in third, Ishizaki was in fourth.

"*Huff huff.* Take it, Ayanokouji! Go for first!" he shouted, handing the baton over.

Whether we took first would come down to Kouenji, but I took the baton and ran.

"I'll kill ya if ya hold back!" shouted Ishizaki with the last of his strength, before collapsing to the ground.

His exhaustion was natural, considering he'd run more than three kilometers on a mountain path. I decided to slowly but surely close the gap with the runners in front. I ran a little bit faster than everyone else, making sure not to disrupt my breathing. Rather than trying to go on the offense right off the bat pace, I waited for their stamina to drain before overtaking them. By doing that, I fooled them into thinking I'd passed because they were too slow.

Despite the bumpy terrain, two kilometers wasn't enough to leave me out of breath. Just like that, I overtook one runner ahead of me, putting me in third, only a short distance behind the second-place runner. Then I handed the baton off to Kouenji.

Nine people had handled this baton. Our fate was in this man's hands.

"Now then. Let's work up a light sweat, shall we?"

Kouenji, brushing back his hair, took the baton in hand and ran with a nonchalant look on his face. He probably wasn't going at full speed, but he was quite fast. If he kept to that speed, we'd probably be fine. That was, of course, so long as he didn't slow to a stroll once he was out of sight.

In the end, despite all the anxiety he'd caused us, Kouenji wound up finishing in second place. I didn't know if he couldn't overtake the runner in first or if he simply didn't want to. Probably the latter.

The speeches we'd have to give after this intense race were going to be hell for the first-years. We'd have to speak at length in raised voices after completely exhausting ourselves.

However, nothing particularly noteworthy occurred. While I had some doubts about Kouenji's somewhat... let's say *dramatic* performance during his speech, everyone seemed to have completed the assignment without any real difficulty.

9.3

. . . .

A ND SO, the longest day of the special exam was over.
The majority of our group—no, of the entire student
body—was totally exhausted. I had no doubt that our
group would score much higher than we'd initially expected. If this came down to what the average scores were,
then our group had a good chance to finish strong. The
rest came down to how well Nagumo's group and the
third-years scored, but I was certain we wouldn't score
below the threshold set by the school.

As on the first day, all the male students assembled
inside the gymnasium, shortly joined by the female students. They were probably going to announce the results
for both the guys and girls. It was already five o'clock in
the evening—safe to assume it would be late by the time
we made it back to school.

"You've all done excellent work at this camp school these past eight days. Though the exact nature of the contents differ, of course, this special exam is held every few years. Overall, you performed better than the students from the previous exam. I suppose that's down to your good teamwork," announced an elderly man I'd never seen before. He smiled the whole time he spoke.

I was guessing he was the person in charge of the camp.

"I will announce the results, but first, I must say that the boys couldn't have had a better finish. They all successfully met the school's standards, and thus there will be zero boys expelled."

The moment he announced that, I heard the relieved murmurs of several boys.

"Whew, no one's getting expelled," said Keisei, putting his hand to his chest with a sigh of relief. Ishizaki lightly smacked him on the back.

"Never once thought we'd get expelled from the start. We were aimin' for first, after all."

"Yeah."

No matter our personal feelings, avoiding expulsion was significant. However, the way the elderly man phrased that announcement was slightly concerning. If no one from the entire student body was getting expelled, he'd have no reason to specify "boys" the way he'd just done.

Which meant...

"Now then. I will announce the overall winner among the boys' large groups, but I will only be reading the name of the third-year student acting as representative. Points for the students placed in that group, which includes first-through third-year students, will be given at a later date."

With that, the elderly man slowly read the names aloud.

"Third-year Class C Ninomiya Kuranosuke-kun's group took first place."

When that announcement was made, some third-year students immediately began to cheer. For a moment, I didn't know whose group that was, but then realized it was the large group that Horikita's brother was in. It would seem he'd won his battle against Nagumo.

"Well done, Horikita. Just what I'd expect of you."

Fujimaki praised Horikita's brother, ignoring the rest of the announcements. The groups that came in second place and below were announced, but from the senior students' point of view, this was nothing more than a bonus.

"Hey, Yukimura. We got second. We did it!"

"Yeah, I'm glad. I'm really, really glad."

They didn't announce the actual difference in our scores, but Nagumo's group had come in second place, so I was guessing the margin had been narrow. Everyone seemed to think Nagumo would quiet down a little now that he'd placed second, but honestly, I wasn't sure whose strategy would carry the day in the end.

Why was that? Well, I didn't have anything particular at stake here, but...Nagumo was smiling beside me, showing no sign of being upset at all. That wasn't the look of a man who'd lost after dramatically and defiantly throwing down the gauntlet.

I supposed I expected as much. Expected, in other words, that he was concocting something incredibly evil behind the scenes.

"You've earned first place. Congratulations are in order, Horikita-senpai. Just as I'd expect from you," said Nagumo, speaking loudly.

Horikita didn't offer any kind of response. He simply stayed silent for the rest of the announcements. Maybe he was also beginning to feel something was off about this.

"You lost, Nagumo," said the third-year student Fujimaki, clearly oblivious to what was going on. He probably felt he'd just served a cocky junior student a piece of humble pie.

"It sure seems that way. But they've only just started announcing the results, haven't they?" replied Nagumo.

"Enough already. It's over."

"Sure. For the boys."

"For the boys? Well, yeah, but the girls have nothing to do with this. That was the agreement, wasn't it, Nagumo?"

"Yes. They have nothing to do with the fight between Horikita-*senpai* and I, that's right. At all."

Fujimaki's face turned stern upon hearing Nagumo's enigmatic choice of words. Ishikura, a third-year student from Class B, stood beside Nagumo and listened to the conversation, quietly observing what was happening.

"Next, I would like to announce the results for the girls' groups. First place goes to third-year Class C Ayase Natsu-san's group."

This time, some of the girls let out cheers of joy. The large group that the third-year student named Ayase was in charge of contained a small group composed mostly of first-year Class C students, including Horikita and Kushida. They might have earned quite a few points.

But the joy was short-lived. Something dire came close on its heels.

"Um, well... This is truly regrettable, but unfortunately, there is one small group among the girls that failed to secure the necessary score."

Everyone's faces froze upon hearing that. Even the students who'd been cheering went silent. Everyone had tried their absolute best not to fall below the borderline. However, life can be cruel. Someone was definitely going to be expelled.

Now the only question that remained was: Would be a first-year getting expelled? Or perhaps an upperclassman? Horikita's brother looked over at Nagumo as though he had just noticed something. Like he was trying to discern the meaning behind the cocksure smile that Nagumo had worn on his face this entire time.

However, it was already too late.

"I will first announce the group that came in last place... That would be the group represented by third-year Class B student Ikari Momoko-san."

Just like with the boys, it wasn't immediately clear to me who was included in that group. But the anguished cries from some of the girls began to make things clear. The large group that had come in last place had been decided. Now it was just a matter of which of the small groups within it had fallen below the acceptable threshold. In a worst-case scenario, students from all three grade levels might be expelled at the same time.

"As for the group that fell below the threshold..."

The gymnasium grew even quieter than during *zazen*. Everyone's eyes were focused on the old man's mouth, desperate to know the results.

"It is also..."

The gymnasium was divided into two camps: those who continued smiling, and those who were getting nervous.

"The group Ikari Momoko-san represents. That is all."

The moment the old man declared the results, Nagumo started laughing happily, as if he had been holding it in until now. The passage of time, which had slowed to a trickle, started to flow normally once more. However, many of the students didn't seem to understand what was happening. Why was Nagumo laughing because some student he didn't even know was going to be ordered to leave the school?

One student from third-year Class B was going to be expelled. But he was laughing because...that wasn't all there was to this.

"What did you do, Nagumo?!" shouted Fujimaki, who now understood what was going on. He closed in on Nagumo.

Horikita's brother didn't approach Nagumo, but he wore a grim look.

"Come now, *senpai*, we're still in the middle of the results. Please calm down. This has nothing to do with you anyway, Fujimaki-*senpai*. Does it? The only thing that's happening is that a Class B student will be expelled.

If anything, this means you'll pull even further ahead of your rivals, right?" Nagumo snickered.

"Um, please, some quiet, if you would. Now, it is truly unfortunate, but this means Ikari-san will have to take responsibility for the group, and thus, she will be expelled. Ikari-san may also decide to invoke the solidarity rule and name someone else within her group. Ikari-san, please consult with me later. Next, I will announce which of the girls' groups has taken second place."

Despite saying that it was unfortunate, he continued speaking, solemnly. But Horikita's brother no longer cared about getting first place himself. He'd fallen for the trap set for him, just like Nagumo had intended. It was precisely because Horikita Manabu was an upstanding, honorable individual that he'd got beaten by Nagumo Miyabi, who'd struck from where you'd least expect it.

"Ayanokouji, why is Fujimaki-*senpai* so angry...? Just like Nagumo-*senpai* said, the representative is a student from Class B. Isn't this a boon for Class A?" Keisei whispered into my ear.

"No, the problem isn't the representative. I think it's who's going down with her."

"Huh?"

We were ordered to disband. While they prepped the buses for our return trip, we were given free time to change. Nagumo stood his ground proudly. He called one of the girls over.

"Ikari-*senpai*. I'm sure everyone is wondering just who in the world will be expelled alongside you."

The third-year Class B girl named Ikari, who was slated for expulsion, was calm. If anything, it was the other girls in her small group, which was mostly composed of students from Class B and Class D, who looked worried.

I knew what was going to happen. I was certain of it, thanks to the information I'd gotten from Asahina and Kei.

And among the people in that group...there was one single participant from A Class: Tachibana Akane. I looked over at Horikita's brother and slowly spoke to him inside my mind.

Look, I get it. To ensure that you all graduated from Class A, and also to counter Nagumo, you instructed every Class A student, both guys and girls, not to take on the role of representative. Didn't you? Because as long as you produced solid scores, none of you would get expelled.

However, you knew that wasn't an airtight defense. That was why you accepted Nagumo's challenge, making sure to set the conditions that the fight be above the board, in an attempt to defend against his malice. You also avoided making any imprudent contact with the girls, hoping to lower the risk of Nagumo exploiting that opening and targeting them.

You exhausted every measure available to you, and still kept things civil, I'll grant you that. But even so, Nagumo's malice knows no bounds. I don't need to say much more about that, though.

This special exam was a trap that Nagumo had set without even the school realizing it. The people who had gotten caught in his trap understood the situation they were in now. Their faces had gone so pale that it looked like they might collapse any moment.

"Well, isn't that obvious? It's the student who made sure our group knew no peace. Tachibana Akane-san, from Class A," spat Ikari angrily, speaking loud enough for everyone to hear.

"Nagumo... You promised Horikita that you wouldn't involve any third parties in this, didn't you?" shouted Fujimaki. He rounded on Nagumo, getting in his face, like he was about to start throwing punches.

"Please wait. This has nothing to do with me."

"That's a bald-faced lie!"

Fujimaki was furious, and it was obvious why. No one here was fooled. Nagumo had known what was going on.

"Well, I'll go notify the school who I'll be dragging down with me," announced Ikari indifferently, heading off toward the instructor. Her classmate Ishikura went with her, nestling close.

No one could do anything to stop what was happening. Even Hashimoto recognized that.

"Tachibana-senpai dragged down Ikari-senpai's group," he said. "As a result, their group's score fell below the average, so she's being taken down as well via the solidary rule. That's all there is to it, isn't it?"

Unlike Fujimaki, Horikita's brother called over to Tachibana, who stood still, before he approached Nagumo. Some of the third-year students walked away, the looks on their faces indicating that they couldn't even bring themselves to say anything in the current situation.

"Horikita-kun, I'm sorry...!"

"Tachibana, why didn't you consult with me sooner? Surely you should have noticed something was amiss."

"That's because...I knew that you would take the burden upon yourself, Horikita-kun..." said Tachibana, apologizing, in tears.

She likely hadn't noticed at first. How she'd been caught in a trap from the moment the groups were decided. But as time passed, she must have sensed something was wrong...sensed that the group she had been placed in was created for the sole purpose of taking down Tachibana Akane.

And still, she'd faced the exam, working as hard as she could in hopes of a miracle. But as you might expect, reality was cruel. Still, Tachibana should have been prepared to accept this. Even if she was expelled, it would only cost Class A one hundred class points.

"Ah, such beautiful friendship. Or perhaps I should call it love? Anyway, congratulations to you, Horikita-senpai. Once again, please allow me to pay you my compliments. I've lost."

A loser would never speak in the tone of voice Nagumo did now. I doubted there was a single person here who believed what he said.

"It was a truly fantastic strategy. No, perhaps I should say that it was a strategy that went well beyond what is expected. There is not a single person here who can read my intentions, and that includes you, Horikita-senpai," said Nagumo. He laughed loudly, not ceasing his attacks on his injured opponent. "Please, enlighten me, Tachibana-*senpai*. How does it feel to have served on the student council, to have been on verge of graduating from Class A, only to then be expelled? And Horikita-senpai, how do you feel right now? I'm sure you must be positively *filled* with feelings of frustration, the likes of which you've never felt before. Hmm?"

After hearing what Nagumo said, Horikita sighed quietly.

"Why didn't you go after me?" he asked.

"Because I can't imagine you ever being expelled, even if I tried such a method on you, senpai. I was terrified you'd counter me with some method I couldn't anticipate. But more importantly, I've never actually wanted you to be expelled, Horikita-senpai. If anything, if you got expelled, then we wouldn't be able to see each other, would we? That's why, of all the many possible targets, I went after Tachibana-senpai. I wanted to see your face when I made her disappear," said Nagumo. He laughed as he said it, as though implying he'd done it purely for curiosity's sake, or on a whim.

"I understand that we have very different principles, but I trusted you. Regarding the matter of competition, I had thought you were a man capable of facing me directly, head-to-head. It would appear that I was wrong," said Horikita.

Nagumo apparently took no offense to this.

"Trust is an awful lot like experience points in a game," he said. "The more you accumulate, the more you increase your worth. I think that the ultimate form of this is family. If you ran into a stranger when you were out and about at night, you'd be cautious. But if that person happened to be family, then you'd drop your guard. It's like that, Horikita-senpai. Though I feel you don't like me very much, I've managed to gain a certain degree of your trust over these past two years. Even though our values were different, I've always done everything that I said I would do. I followed your instructions and stuck to the rules. That being said, you *are* a rather canny upperclassman. I'm sure you didn't trust me *completely,* did you?"

It was safe to assume that Nagumo knew the orders that Horikita's brother had issued his class to protect them and collect information.

"However...even if you had your suspicions about me, it wasn't as though you could betray me first, senpai," added Nagumo.

That was the downside of a nonaggressive defense policy.

"You've lost something rather significant because of your curiosity, Nagumo."

"Oh, you mean your trust? I chose to discard that myself. For the sake of trying to gain an understanding of my senpai, who cares so deeply for his juniors."

Nagumo had proven that he cared nothing for promises. He wanted to fight without limiting factors such as trust and respect. That was the kind of challenge he was offering.

"I've come to understand how you do things quite well," said Horikita Manabu.

"I'm glad to hear that. This was, after all, nothing more than a warm-up," replied Nagumo. "I'm fine with getting people expelled, if I have to. That's the way this school operates."

While everyone else panicked, Horikita continued to speak calmly. "You seem to be operating under the impression that Tachibana will be expelled."

"W-wait, Horikita-kun!" Tachibana shouted.

But there was a fierce determination in Horikita's eyes.

"Oh, ho? I thought we were going to end with a draw, both of us losing something. But you're *really* gonna spend all that? I mean, that would mean a lot of money and class points."

Revocation of expulsion. The ultimate tool that anyone could use, as long as they met the requirements.

"Please, don't do this. This is all my fault..."

Tachibana desperately tried to stop Horikita. However, it seemed Fujimaki shared Horikita's opinion, as he addressed Class A.

"We understand. We've made it this far as Class A because we understand it better than anyone else. Isn't that right?"

"That's exactly right, Horikita. No need to hold back. Use it."

Some of their classmates spoke up to voice their support.

"Are you really okay with this, Horikita-senpai? For a third-year class to save a student from expulsion right now would mean essentially giving up your position as Class A, you know?"

"Even if we give up our position, all we need to do is take it back again. As you said, that's how this school operates."

"Is that so? Well, I guess that's fine."

Miyabi was probably going to amicably discuss the strategy he had in mind from this point onward. I already knew what that strategy was. There was no need for me to stay and hang on to every word.

Besides, there was nothing I could do, even if I stayed.

Horikita Suzune had anxiously watched the entire situation unfold, from beginning to end. She was looking so intently at her older brother that she didn't even notice me as I walked away, which was fine by me.

I left the gymnasium. When I did, I saw Kei standing near the entrance, looking like she was waiting for me. As I stepped out into the corridor, she followed a little way behind me.

"Everything happened the way you said it would, Kiyotaka. You seriously knew what was going to happen. You knew Tachibana-senpai would be targeted. I would have thought anyone other than Horikita-senpai would've been fair game for Nagumo to target..."

"It was the rules of the special exam," I said. "As soon as I heard the student council was involved in its planning, I thought this might happen. It's certainly true that anyone could have been targeted. However, Nagumo went through the trouble of setting up a trap this complex. If he wanted to stick the knife in as deep as possible, his targets were limited. The only female student that Horikita had a deep connection with was Tachibana."

That was the conclusion I'd drawn after piecing together information from Kei, Ichinose, and Asahina. Also, there was a clear sense of collusion going on between Nagumo and Ishikura. It was clear those two were connected. Nagumo hadn't just gathered all the second-year students under his wing. He'd also brought all the third-year students who weren't in Class A over to his side.

"I'm sure everyone in the large group colluded to get a low score. The members of Tachibana's small group must've been holding back quite a bit, too. That way, it was simple for them to fall below the threshold."

But Kei didn't seem quite convinced.

"But why did he use Class B? It would've been fine if he put a Class D student in charge as representative. I mean, since he used Class B, that means Horikita-senpai is still in Class A, right? If Nagumo wanted to knock him down to Class B, shouldn't he have gone with a Class D student?"

Kei had a good eye. She was certainly right about that. If that was Nagumo's goal, it would've been an excellent strategy for him to make a Class D student the representative, thereby lessening the gap between Class A and Class B that way. Or so you'd assume, normally.

"It's precisely because it was Class B that this was possible. If Tachibana acquitted her tasks during this special exam without issue, it wouldn't be easy to get her expelled via the solidarity rule. Unless the three classes all came together, the strategy wouldn't be viable. Let's consider third-year Class D. They're the least likely to make it to Class A before graduation, given their current situation. If a student from Class D was the representative, they might decide to name a student from B or C to take down with them in order to move their class up, even if it's just by one level. But it would be pointless to drag down a student from a lower class at this juncture."

On the other hand, if you looked at it from the perspective of Class D or Class C students who *weren't* the representative, they'd probably be happy to help bring down students from Class A and Class B. That was why Ikari's group had banded together to thoroughly demonize Tachibana, making her out to be the bad guy. If anything, they probably blatantly and maliciously harassed her. Tachibana probably hadn't been able to sleep at night.

And as a result, they didn't get good grades in the end. Even if their average grade was mediocre, if it appeared Tachibana had held the group back for the entire week, that would be enough to paint her as a target.

If someone filed a complaint, there would've been a discussion. But if the entire small group conspired to claim that Tachibana had been an obstacle for them in places and in ways that weren't publicly visible, the school would have to recognize that. Of course, it would set a bad precedent, but there would probably be some amendments made to the rules for the next special exam in a few years.

And so Nagumo's elaborate strategy had come together, and he'd successfully laid the way for Tachibana to be expelled.

"But wait, how could he even pull off a strategy like

this? If I were a student in Class B, I sure as hell wouldn't be okay with getting expelled for the sake of my class. What's the payoff?"

"I'm not sure what kind of payoff there was, but Ikari won't be expelled."

"Huh? But she was the representative, wasn't she?"

"They probably predicted Horikita's brother would use that lifeline option. By paying twenty million points and three hundred Class Points, he can revoke a student's expulsion. Because Horikita used that option, Nagumo was okay with Class B using it too."

"Well, now I can't tell what he gained from all this. If anything, isn't it a loss?"

"Spending those class points will sting, but if Class A had to use the same lifeline, the gap between the classes won't widen at all. As far as private points go, this won't hurt them at all."

"So third-year Class B is that rich?"

"No. The ironclad condition of Nagumo's strategy was that he would pay all the private points himself. If he didn't, there's no way they'd cooperate."

Most likely, Nagumo had contacted Ishikura on the bus and paid him the twenty million points in advance. The proof of that could be seen in Ikari's and Ishikura's calm behavior.

"The second-year class is a monolith. If he collected money from the entirety of the second-years, he wouldn't even need fifteen thousand per person. Saving one student from expulsion could be bought on the cheap."

"What a *seriously* insane way of fighting. That is definitely *not* normal."

"That's how Nagumo Miyabi does things. That's all there is to it."

He didn't come up with a strategy after seeing what the exam was like. He came up with a strategy and then created the exam. Class A, led by Horikita's brother, would get stuck with paying twenty million private points in total, as a single class. Quite a bit of damage. They might have to face one or two more special exams before they graduated, and they'd just lost a staggering amount of money.

If Horikita's brother were expelled in the next exam, he wouldn't have enough money to save himself. That lifeline would be dead in the water.

"I think it's time we head our separate ways."

"Wait, one more thing." Kei was persistent. "I can't think of any way to counter the way Nagumo-senpai's thinks. The method he used to set Tachibana-senpai up for expulsion... It's, like, the perfect trap or something. Is that why you didn't make a move, Kiyotaka?"

"It's quite a formidable strategy. Nagumo had a checkmate set up by the time his enemy got in the game."

This was a good precedent to set. Private points could be powerful.

"Say, what if I wind up in the same situation that Tachibana-senpai was in…? In a situation where you can't even use a lifeline? I mean, there'd be nothing you could do at a time like that, right?" asked Kei in a soft voice.

"You don't even need me to answer, do you? I won't let you get expelled. No matter what methods I have to use."

In the end, Horikita Manabu chose to part with Class A's class and private points, thus saving Tachibana Akane. As I'd predicted, Ishikura from Class B did the same to save Ikari. An extremely unusual happenstance: two classes utilizing the lifeline option at the same time.

From this point on, students across all grade levels at the Advanced Nurturing High School were going to be expelled, one after another.

POSTSCRIPT

HEY, IT'S THE GUY who says "Next time *for sure!*" deep within his heart when announcing the next volume, only for it to end up being late again: Kinugasa.

Considering nothing ever goes as planned, even I've started to get annoyed with myself. "I'll release it any day! Any day now!" I always make those announcements, and there's always a delay. Truly terrible, isn't it?

And so I will state clearly and unequivocally: I will stop making declarations about release dates in the postscript.

It's been about seven or eight weeks since I've hurt my fingers, I think? Even though that much time has passed, I'm still a ways off from a full recovery. I'm still receiving treatment and trying to take care of myself, wondering if I can maintain the four-month schedule I've been on until now.

Anyhow, before I even noticed, it was already May. Time really does fly, doesn't it? Time has passed in the blink of an eye, considering it's been a full three years since I first released *Classroom of the Elite*. Back when I was working on volume 1, part of me didn't believe I'd be able to go on selling my works and writing for this long. I'm extremely delighted. But I've also become keenly aware that it's not just my fingers that are aching. My entire body is falling apart. I'm really going to take better care of myself.

In volume 8 of *Classroom*, we started seeing more of the upperclassmen. A wide variety of characters showed up: the good-for-nothings, the shady, and the dependable. I hope you enjoyed reading this volume. And the next volume, volume 9, well, it, nnngh, will c-come out in S-S-Sept...aagghh. No, I've already decided to stop making announcements! Stop!

All right, that's enough of my idiocy. You know, personally, there's one thing I've really wanted for a long time now. I guess you could call it a secret desire. I really want a massage chair. Like, *really, really* want it. But it's expensive. On top of that, it would take up a lot of space that I don't have.

Seriously, I've been agonizing over this for years. In the end, I can't decide. Will I ever buy one? Or will that day never come? Well, no matter how much time passes, I'll continue to write about wanting it and never buy it. If anyone out there knows about some wonderful massage chairs, please tell me about it.